"Come here," I commanded, "and see if you can give me a real kiss!" I held out my arms, but she didn't rush into them as I had hoped. She looked a little tentative and a little scared, but she moved slowly in my direction and actually tilted her face up for my kiss.

I lowered my head, put my arms around her, and closed my mouth over hers. When I pulled away, I asked, "Come on, Sandy, can't you act like you enjoy it?"

"I was enjoying it."

"Kiss me back, okay?" I asked, moving to kiss her again. This time she kissed me in return and I could have stood there all night, just holding her in my arms and kissing her.

Finally I lifted my lips from hers. I just stood there for a while, hugging her. I was getting somewhere! I'd taken her out for a date, I'd even kissed her, and she'd returned the kiss, albeit reluctantly. Why, give me another month and we'd surely be going together!

Dear Readers:

Thank you for your unflagging interest in First Love From Silhouette. Your many helpful letters have shown us that you have appreciated growing and stretching with us, and that you demand more from your reading than happy endings and conventional love stories. In the months to come we will make sure that our stories go on providing the variety you have come to expect from us. We think you will enjoy our unusual plot twists and unpredictable characters who will surprise and delight you without straying too far from the concerns that are very much part of all our daily lives.

We hope you will continue to share with us your ideas about how to keep our books your very First Loves. We depend on you to keep us on our toes!

Nancy Jackson
Senior Editor
FIRST LOVE FROM SILHOUETTE

AND MILES TO GO
Beverly Sommers

First Love from Silhouette

Published by Silhouette Books New York

America's Publisher of Contemporary Romance

First Loves by Beverly Sommers

BEVERLY SOMMERS grew up in Evanston, Illinois, and went on to college in California, graduating with a major in English. Subsequently she has studied law, taught fifth grade, been a counselor in Juvenile Hall and owned an art gallery. She has lived in Spain and Greece and currently makes her home in New York.

Chapter One

I first saw Sandy in September of my senior year, and my first impression of her was that she was a boy.

It was after school and I was working out with the track team. I was circling the track at a pretty good pace, in fact I would say at a very good pace, when this skinny kid streaked by me as if I was standing still. This kind of annoyed me, not only because someone was able to streak by me, but because it turned out to be some kid who was giving me competition, and not just one of the guys.

I picked up my pace—not by much, since I was already running almost full out—but by that time the kid was so far ahead of me, there was no possibility of catching up. I gave a mental shrug, saying to myself that whoever it was had probably started out right behind me and was practicing for the hundred-yard dash.

That hope was dashed when not more than a minute later the same slight form once again raced by me. I got a good

enough look this time to see that the kid's running was
flawless, I'd even say effortless. Whoever it was, if he was
going to be on the track team this year, we'd have it made.
We had a pretty good team anyway, but someone like that
could get us a lot of added attention. We had a solid team,
but we'd never really had a star.

I finished my laps and headed over to talk to the coach.
We were pretty informal with him and called him Zabo,
which was short for his unpronounceable last name. He was
a good guy, fairly young, and he'd broken a couple of records in his time, which made us respect him even more than
we would have anyway for just being a good coach.

"Who *is* he?" were my first words to Zabo as the kid
whizzed by once more.

"Her."

I was sure I had misunderstood him. "What?"

He grinned at me. "I said it was a her. A female. Just a
kid, actually. She's only fourteen."

"Fastest girl I've ever seen," I told him.

"She just could be the fastest girl anyone's ever seen."

I looked at him to see if he was kidding around, but Zabo
never kids around when it comes to track. And she was fast,
I had to admit it. But the fastest girl of all time? That
seemed a little hard to believe. Not that there didn't have to
be a fastest girl somewhere, but that she just happened to
show up at Wilson High seemed too good to be true.

I was kind of glad in a way that if we had a star on the
team she'd be competing against other girls and not breaking records with me coming in second or third or even
worse. I don't mind competition, but I'd rather it came from
my own sex. This is my personal viewpoint—it doesn't
happen to go down so well with my girlfriend Michelle, but
that's life. There's something about a girl beating me at
anything that doesn't go down so well with me.

"What races are you going to run her in?" I asked Zabo, seeing as he was in a talkative mood. Sometimes he just grunts when you ask him anything, but today he was being downright loquacious.

"None," he muttered, and again I thought I'd heard him wrong. Maybe it was one of his grunts and I just thought he'd said *none*.

"Is she a miler?"

"Among other things. She's just going to work out with us, she's not a member of the team."

"Why not?" I didn't think it was possible that she hadn't made the team.

"She'll be competing nationally, that's why not. She'll be working out with us, but then she goes over to Runners West for another workout. The coach over there's going to be entering her in all the big meets." He sighed and pushed his hair back off his forehead. "A chance in a lifetime, and I don't get her. Oh, well, I guess I'll just have to be satisfied with you guys."

He motioned the girl off the track, and then, as she ran over to him, I moved off a distance so I could get a good look at her without her noticing. I have to admit I was intrigued: it wasn't every day I got this close to a track star.

The word "star" makes you think of someone glamorous, but there was nothing glamorous about her. She was short and very slim, in fact her slimness was the first thing you noticed about her. Like all good runners she didn't look as though she had an ounce of body fat on her, just all lean bones and tight skin. Plus, she had no figure, less than my sister Chrissie, who's only in the seventh grade. Her face was ordinary, her light brown hair cut shorter than some of the boys' hair on the team, and she just pushed it back from her small face. I couldn't see her eyes too well but they appeared to be a washed-out blue, maybe gray.

She was the kind of girl I wouldn't give a second look at in the halls or in one of my classes, and yet, knowing what I did about her, I found her fascinating. I really loved track, and I figured if she was as good as Zabo said, she might turn out to be one of the greats. And that kind of talent I find intriguing.

I went back onto the track and did a series of some middle-distance turns. After that, it was time to head for the showers, and as I belatedly remembered, I'd promised to pick up Michelle after her dentist's appointment.

I headed toward the gym with Kenny Allen, who'd become my best friend during the past year. He was our ace long jumper and had broken the high-school record early on in his junior year. Unfortunately, at the end of last year someone broke his record, but that's the way it goes.

"Did you see her?" I asked him once we were past the others and couldn't be overheard.

"You mean that little thing with U.S.A. on her chest instead of Wilson?"

I nodded.

"What I could see of her, man. She went by me so fast it was hard to get a good look."

"Zabo thinks she might be the fastest female runner in the world."

"Yeah, that was my impression, too. She's also faster than any of the males we've got."

"Do you know her name?" I asked him.

"Nope—all I know about is her speed, and that's awesome."

"She's working out with us, but she's running for Runners West," I told him.

"You sound like you're sorry. I wouldn't think it would do much for your macho image to be beaten by a little bit of a thing like her," he teased me. His girlfriend was a hurdler and although he always claimed he liked competitive girls, I noticed he hadn't picked a long jumper to go out with.

I couldn't get the girl out of my mind while I showered: it wasn't until Kenny flicked his towel at my rear end that I came out of my reverie. I'd been standing around naked for several minutes I guess, and suddenly I saw that everyone but me was already dressed. I got into my Levi's and T-shirt and was tying my running shoes when Kenny asked if I wanted to go to the beach and play some volleyball.

"I promised Michelle I'd pick her up," I told him, following him out to the parking lot.

"Talk to you tonight, then," he said, heading in the direction of his green Toyota.

I have an old Mustang that's lousy on mileage but great on speed, which might be one of the reasons I get such bad mileage. There's something about being next to a car at a stoplight that makes me want to race, and I can seldom resist the temptation. Most of the time I beat the other car, too, but I don't know whether that's because I'm faster or because the other driver doesn't feel like wasting his gas.

I tossed my books in the back seat and opened all the windows to let in some air. The books were window dressing so my folks would figure I had studying to do. They get suspicious when I don't bring home books, even though this early in the year we don't have all that much studying to do. Anyway, I'm one of those people who study for an exam at the last minute. I figure if I started studying any earlier I'd just forget it all by the time the test came around anyway. Mostly I spend the time when I'm supposedly studying on the phone with either Michelle or Kenny, and since my parents are downstairs, usually with the TV on, they never know the difference. Chrissie knows what I'm up to, but she'd never tell on me.

Michelle's dentist was in downtown Long Beach, and I wasn't looking forward to finding a parking spot anywhere near there, but when I got to the building Michelle was waiting on the sidewalk and had saved me the trouble.

Michelle was a junior at that time and we had been going together about a year and a half. The first thing anyone notices about Michelle is her looks, and if I were rating her I'd have to say she'd be very close to a ten. She's got dark brown hair that's so long she can sit on it, the biggest brown eyes I've ever seen, and a figure that gets so many looks from other guys that I'm always telling her to wear looser clothes. It's not that she wears tight clothes, though; it's just that on her you notice the body before you notice the clothes.

Take what she was wearing that day, for instance. She was just wearing jeans and a pink shirt, which was probably what half the girls in school were wearing, but on her the outfit looked like it should be illegal. I don't know, maybe I'm exaggerating. Maybe it was just that I liked her so much that I thought she looked great. But in a year and half I sure hadn't become tired of looking at her.

She got into the car and gave me a quick kiss, then made a face so I'd ask her what was wrong.

"I'm numb, that's what's wrong. He gave me so much Novocain I can't even feel my mouth."

"So don't get Novocain if you don't like it."

"I like pain even less." She turned on my radio, which for once I'd forgotten to do myself, and I tried to get out of Long Beach fast before the rush-hour traffic started.

I headed down toward Belmont Shore and ended up in the parking lot of Hamburger Henry's. I didn't think a little bit of Novocain would put Michelle off eating. She liked to eat even more than I did.

We sat at one of the outside tables. Hamburger Henry has these telephones on the tables for you to call in your order, and then a waiter brings it. Michelle never gets tired of calling in orders and we both never get tired of the food there. It costs more than McDonald's, but it's worth it.

I was sitting there looking at Michelle and thinking how pretty she was while at the same time the image of that small girl kept flashing through my mind. You've got to understand that at that point I wasn't thinking of her as a girl—I was just as impressed when I'd thought she was a boy. I was remembering her phenomenal speed and wondering what it would feel like to be so impressive at that age. I would never really know, though, because at fourteen I hadn't been impressive at all, not in any way. I was only about five-five and too skinny and really shy around girls. My running speed hadn't been any big deal then, either. Now I was almost six feet tall and had filled out some, although running kept me pretty slim, and I hadn't been shy around girls for a long time. In fact, Michelle wished I were shyer in that regard and was always accusing me of flirting with her friends. There's just something about me that makes me want to be nice to pretty girls, and most high-school girls look pretty to me.

"Why aren't you talking? I'm the one with the numb mouth."

I reached across the table and took Michelle's hand. "Sorry, I was just thinking about track."

"You taking me to the dance Saturday night?"

"Not if I can get out of it."

"You can't."

I shrugged. "Then I guess I'm taking you." I hated dancing and school dances, but since Michelle hated football and we'd be seeing the game before the dance, I figured it was a compromise on both our parts. Anyway, I wouldn't have to really dance except maybe a couple of slow ones with Michelle, and dancing close with Michelle was something I didn't object to. The rest of the time she'd dance with her girlfriends and I could talk to some of the guys. Not Kenny, though; he genuinely liked dancing. Of course he's black and they're good dancers. That's only a joke, something I tease him about. Actually, some of them, particularly the football players, can't dance at all. But I've got to say that Kenny dances every bit as well as he long jumps.

I guess I lapsed into silence again because the next thing I knew Michelle was saying, "All right, what was so momentous about track today that you can't talk?"

I felt a little guilty when she said that, but then our hamburgers arrived and I got out of talking for another few minutes. But, "I asked you a question," she reminded me as I was chewing my last bite.

I took a long swallow of my Coke before answering her. "There was this girl working out with us..."

"I should've known!" She gave me one of her long-suffering looks as if to say I couldn't even be trusted on track.

I decided to let her have it. "Yeah," I said, a smirk on my face, "I've never seen anything like her." Which so far was the truth. "She's this gorgeous blonde, really built, you know what I mean?"

She looked like she knew exactly what I meant.

"I didn't talk to her or anything, I don't even know her name..."

"But you will, I'm sure," she snapped. It was going past teasing and I could tell she was really getting jealous.

"Hey, Michelle—I'm only kidding. There *was* a girl, but she's only fourteen and looks more like twelve. My sister's sexier-looking than she is, believe me."

She looked somewhat mollified. "So what's so great about her?"

"Her speed."

Her eyes took on a familiar gleam. "You mean she's faster than *you*?"

"It sure looked that way."

"Good. About time some girl beat you at something."

"She's not going to beat me at anything because we don't compete against the girls."

"Then maybe it's about time you did."

"You'll have to take that up with the track officials, but I don't think they're going to change the way things are done."

"What *does* she look like?"

"I don't know. Small, colorless—I never would've even noticed her if she hadn't gone by me so fast."

"I swear, Tom—if she turns out to be some gorgeous blonde...."

"You know I prefer gorgeous brunettes," I told her, and in fact, that was the truth. Everyone in my family's a blonde, which is probably why I go for brunettes. I don't think I could be interested in a girl who looked like she might be my sister. All the girls I've been interested in have had dark hair, although Michelle is the only girl I've really gone with.

I left my car in the parking lot and we walked down to the beach. It was almost dinnertime, and the place was pretty deserted except for a few little kids who'd probably been stuffing themselves with junk food and wanted to postpone dinner for as long as possible. My mom thinks I don't eat enōugh, but she doesn't see what I manage to put away when she's not around.

Michelle and I sat down on the wall and I put my arm around her and started kissing her, but she pulled away and said she still couldn't feel anything, so I gave it up. I wasn't much in the mood for kissing anyway, but when you're going with a girl it becomes expected of you. If a day goes by and I don't kiss her at least once she thinks I don't love her anymore and gets upset. I'm not even sure I do love her, but that's another thing that's expected when you go with a girl. When she says she loves you, then you better answer back the same way or you find yourself without a girl-friend. I don't think it makes a whole lot of sense, but I didn't make up the rules.

I go along with all this because I really do like Michelle. She's not only pretty, but she's also fun to be with and can be really funny at times. Going with her is also convenient because she lives just two blocks over from me. When my car breaks down, which happens quite a bit, I can just walk over and see her. Of course now that she's sixteen and has her driver's license, she'll probably be getting her own car one of these days. I think her parents plan on holding out and making it a Christmas present.

When I got home my mom told me that dinner was ready and would I find Chrissie. I went upstairs and saw the door to my room was closed; sure enough, Chrissie was in there on my bed talking on the phone. I like having the upstairs extension in my room, but I don't like having Chrissie in my room. No matter how many times I lecture her on privacy, she's still a snoop, which means I can't leave anything in my room that I don't want her to find.

Her eyes got really wide when she saw me, and she put her hand over the mouthpiece. "Can't I have any privacy?" she asked in this long-suffering voice.

"Mom said to tell you dinner's ready."

She said something softly into the phone in this phony, sweet voice that told me she had to be talking to a boy. It amazes me how many boys call her up. When I was in the seventh grade it wouldn't have occurred to me to call a girl, except when a bunch of us guys got together sometimes and called all the most popular girls and then hung up on them. I guess kids are growing up faster these days.

I was wondering how I was going to eat again so soon but it turned out to be spaghetti so there was no problem. I can always eat spaghetti.

Having Chrissie growing up takes a lot of the pressure off me. It used to be I got questioned a lot at the dinner table, but now it was usually Chrissie who was in the hot seat. That night, Chrissie was being questioned about a party she wanted to go to on Saturday night. I could see my folks thought she was a little young to be going to mixed parties already, but I could also see they were going to let her go. Dad usually lets Chrissie get away with murder anyway, but it really surprised me when Mom said she'd gone to parties in the seventh grade so she guessed it was all right. It made me wonder what they did at parties in the old days.

I decided I'd try to keep an eye on Chrissie that year since my parents were obviously going to let her do anything she wanted. She had a tendency to be a little wild and I didn't want her to turn out to be one of those girls that the boys talk about. And I'd only have this year to get her on the right track because after that I'd be away at college. I was going to start right in after dinner with a lecture, but Chrissie foiled me by disappearing to her best friend's house.

When I talked to Michelle on the phone that night I started to tell her about my worries concerning Chrissie, but she just laughed them off.

"What's the big deal, Tom? I went steady in the seventh grade."

She seemed to have forgotten that I didn't like to hear that kind of talk from her. It always made me mad that Michelle had so much more experience than I did. I think she must have kissed a dozen guys before we started going together. I'd only kissed two girls before her, and neither of them were anything to brag about. Of course I didn't tell her I'd only kissed two other girls. I let her think I'd been around a little, too.

After I hung up with Michelle I tried to get Kenny but his line was busy. Then when I tried again I found that Chrissie was on the downstairs phone, so I gave it up for the night and watched some TV. My mind wasn't really on it, though. I was still thinking about that small girl who'd passed me so fast on the track.

The rest of the week I kept an eye on her during track workouts, but I never got to talk to her. I don't even know what I would have said if I had talked to her. I asked some of the other guys if they knew her name, but no one did. I could have asked Zabo, but then he would've thought I was interested in her and started making jokes about it, and I didn't want that.

I guess I must have been talking about her a lot because Kenny finally said to me, "Do I sense a personal interest in that little girl?"

"What are you, crazy?" I asked him.

"It looks to me like you're the one who's crazy. You got a real nice girlfriend—you don't want to be looking around."

"I'm just impressed by her speed, that's all. She's not even good-looking, Kenny."

"Well, now, that would depend what type you go for. Personally, I think she's real cute."

"Give me a break, she's only a kid."

Kenny gave me a knowing look and refused to be drawn into an argument. Which was frustrating, because I found that I wanted to keep talking about her and he was the only one I could talk to.

On Saturday, I looked for her at the football game and later at the dance but I didn't see her. I was kind of surprised because the dance was the first one of the year, and usually all the freshmen went to kind of get acquainted with everyone else. Our team had won the game, which made the dance even livelier than it would have been if we'd lost, and judging by all the unfamiliar faces, every other freshman in the school had shown up.

Michelle was dancing with one of her friends, and Kenny was out on the floor with his girlfriend. I was stuck in a conversation with Jannine, who was Michelle's best friend. Or at least she thought she was her best friend. What Michelle didn't know and what I didn't tell her was that every chance Jannine got she was coming on to me really strong, and I didn't know what to do about it. She'd only do it when Michelle wasn't around; when she was, Jannine acted as cool as could be. Sometimes I wanted to tell Michelle, because I didn't think best friends ought to do things like that to each other, but I was afraid she'd blame me for it. Which wasn't the case. Jannine was a good-looking blonde, but she was a lot too predatory for my taste. When I'm interested in a girl, I like to be the one to make the first move.

Jannine was trying to get me on the dance floor, which she should have known was a lost cause. I was busy ignoring her and looking around to see if the little runner had shown up yet. I finally decided she hadn't and was ready to call it a night, but the dance hadn't been going on all that long and I knew there wasn't a chance of getting Michelle to leave so early.

Finally, a slow tune came on and Michelle came off the dance floor. Jannine disappeared and I danced my first dance with Michelle. She put her arms around me and rested her head on my shoulder. Usually, I liked dancing with her like that, but this night I just couldn't get into it and I found myself thinking of everything in the world but Michelle. She must have sensed it because I could feel her body stiffen as she moved away from me and looked me in the eye.

"What's gotten into you, Tom?"

"I don't know, I guess I'm just tired."

"I wouldn't kill you if you danced with Jannine, you know."

"What are you talking about?"

"I saw you talking to her."

"She was doing all the talking." I was hoping she was finally getting around to seeing what Jannine was up to.

"It didn't look that way to me."

I tried to pull her close again but she arched her back away from me and kept staring at me in the eyes. "I have no interest whatsoever in Jannine," I told her truthfully.

"Look, I trust her—she's my best friend."

Some best friend, I was thinking. "Michelle, if I wanted to dance with Jannine, I'd dance with her. Let's just drop it, okay?"

"Well, something's gotten into you and I'd like to know what."

"I'm just tired, all right?"

She gave me a doubtful look, but then she put her head back on my shoulder and I kissed the top of her head like I usually do, and I felt her relax in my arms. I didn't want Michelle getting mad at me, it was just too much trouble getting a girlfriend to begin with to mess things up for no reason. And there wasn't any reason; not yet, at least.

After the dance we all went to Hamburger Henry and afterward, when I drove Michelle home, she asked me if I wanted to come in for a while. I knew if I said no I was going to be in big trouble, so I went inside and we watched an old movie on the TV in her family room, and during commercials we kissed a lot, but my heart wasn't really in it and I think she knew that but didn't want to start another argument with me. We made plans to go to a movie the next day and then I was finally able to go home.

I didn't get to sleep very fast that night because I was wondering if I was getting tired of Michelle already. I had always figured I would go with her until I went to college, but the thrill of being with her seemed to be wearing off. I didn't know whether it was always like that if you went with a girl for a long time, or whether it was me. I finally gave up thinking about it and just went to sleep.

I was the first one up the next morning, and I went downstairs and brought the Sunday paper inside. There were only two sections I was interested in, the sports section and the one that listed which movies were playing. I looked at the movie section first because that wouldn't take as long, and I saw that the new Superman movie was on in Lakewood. It might take a little buttering up to get Michelle to go to that one, but I figured I could talk her into it.

I took the sports section out to the kitchen and poured myself some orange juice, then sat down at the table to read it. The first page was devoted mainly to the Dodgers and Angels, but when I turned to the second page I got the surprise of my life. There, in black and white, was a picture of the little runner I'd been spending so much time thinking about.

Local high-school kids seldom get their picture in the *Los Angeles Times*, so at first I thought I must be imagining it was her, but underneath the picture it said she was fourteen-year-old Sandy Smith who had won the mile at some Amateur Athletic Union meet in L.A. the day before.

I kept looking at her picture and saying her name over and over in my mind. Then I read the article about the meet and when it finally mentioned her it said that at five feet and ninety pounds she was already ranked as one of the best female runners in the country. I had to be impressed—anyone would have been impressed. Heck, even the sports writer seemed to be impressed. Here was a kid I'd run around the track with and she had her picture in the paper and was already famous.

I wanted to tear the picture out of the paper and take it up to my room to look at it, but I knew my dad would have a fit if I messed up the section before he's had a chance to read it.

Instead, I went up to my room and looked her up in the phone book. At least I tried to. There was practically an entire page of "Smiths," so I finally gave it up as a lost cause.

I don't know. She was just an ordinary-looking girl with a very ordinary name, but something about her was really getting to me. If I had been smart I would've just forgotten all about her there and then.

Chapter Two

It was October before I got up my nerve to speak to her.

I'm usually not shy around girls, not like I was when I was younger. If I'd had no interest in her I probably would have spoken to her much sooner, but the fact that I now had her picture hidden in my room and spent so much time thinking about her made me hesitate to start up a conversation. Also, the whole thing was making me feel very disloyal to Michelle. The time I usually spent thinking about Michelle was now spent wondering about Sandy.

I'd been acting really crazy, not like me at all. I even tried following her home from school one day. I waited out by the track field in my car until her mother picked her up and then I attempted to keep a distance behind them in order to find out where she lived. But I lost them in the traffic on Pacific Coast Highway. I did memorize the number on the license plate, but that information wouldn't do me any good as I didn't know anyone in the Motor Vehicle Department who could look it up for me.

Naturally, we didn't have any classes together and I never ran across her in the halls, but once I had seen her in the cafeteria at lunch time. She was sitting all by herself and I could see that all she was eating was yogurt and a carton of milk. In a rash move, I got myself a carton of yogurt, but I found it didn't really fill me up—although it didn't taste as bad as I thought it would.

I didn't sit with her, of course, but when I saw her leave the cafeteria I followed her. She just went in the girls' bathroom, though, so I went back to finish my yogurt, then went back in line and got a couple of sandwiches.

Kenny, being quick, didn't miss the action. "If you're so hung up on her why don't you talk to her?" he asked me.

"What're you talking about, Kenny?"

"You know what I'm talking about. That little girl, that's what I'm talking about."

"Call her Sandy, and she's not a little girl."

"All right, don't jump on me just because you lack the guts. I don't know what you see in her, but obviously you see something, so why don't you go for it?"

I had to do something soon, I knew that. I was starting to act just like my little sister. The day I found myself writing her name inside my calculus book I knew I had it bad. I couldn't remember ever writing Michelle's name anywhere, and if Kenny had seen that he would have said I lacked class. And he would have been right.

Also things with Michelle and I were really deteriorating. Michelle's no dummy, and she knew things were getting bad between us. We seemed to spend most our time together arguing. Neither of us seemed ready to break it off, even though I was sometimes tempted. But it just wouldn't have made sense as there was nothing to break it off for. I might be interested in Sandy, but she sure showed no interest in me, if she even knew I was alive. And even if she did show an interest, I just couldn't see going out with a freshman. Some of the senior guys did, but that was only when the freshman in question looked and acted older than her age. This one acted younger and looked all of twelve.

I finally got up my nerve and got my act together, or maybe I was just so desperate by then that I had to hear her voice, but in any case, one Friday, when I was rounding the track, I saw her standing off to the side and I found myself pulling up next to her and stopping.

I tried to be cool. I spent a minute getting my breath back and watching the runners along with her, and then I turned to her and asked, "You coming out to our meet tomorrow night?" She hadn't been to one yet, but I figured she liked track so it didn't seem like a dumb thing to ask.

She looked at me then for the first time and it was really strange. Most girls look at a boy in a different way than they do at a girl, but Sandy didn't. I could have been a tree for all the expression on her face. I think she was the first girl I'd talked to in a long time who didn't smile at me.

"No," she said. That's all, just no. She had a small, soft voice that seemed to go with the rest of her and I wanted to hear her speak again.

"Ah, come on—you'd raise the morale of the team, you know." She'd raised mine, anyway.

She looked at me again, her eyes serious beneath level brows. "I can't, I've got a meet on Saturday."

She had a breathy little way of talking that really got to me. And it wasn't put on or anything. It was as though she didn't want to expend any energy on anything but running.

"Yeah? Where're you running?" I asked her.

"San Diego."

"The mile?"

She nodded. "I'm going to get to enter the 880, too." She was beginning to show a little enthusiasm but I didn't know whether it was because she was talking to me or because she was talking about track. I had a feeling it was the latter. I don't think I'd ever talked to a girl in my life who'd acted so disinterested in me. I was beginning to wonder if maybe I smelled or something and I moved a little bit away from her.

"Well, good luck," I said, and she just nodded again, then went back out on the track and started running. Feeling like a fool, I got back on the track, too.

After practice I drove Kenny home since his car was in the shop. The first thing he said to me was, "I see you finally got brave."

"Very funny."

He obviously thought it was, because he started laughing. "So, you going out with her?"

"Knock it off, Kenny."

"I'm just interested in what progress you're making, that's all."

"Look, I just admire her as a runner, okay?"

"Tell me another one."

"Anyway, as far as I know I'm still going with Michelle."

"I was wondering when you'd remember that."

Things weren't boding well for what I was going to ask him next, but I went ahead anyway. I let about a minute of silence go by and then I said, "Hey, Kenny, you want to go down to San Diego on Saturday?"

"What for?"

"To see a meet."

He was looking at me and just kind of nodding his head up and down. "Yeah, well, I might consider that. I'd like to see her in action myself."

"I don't know where it is exactly."

"It'll be in the papers. You driving?"

I nodded. "Look, I figure we'll be back in time for the game."

"I'd rather see an AAU meet than a football game."

The thing was, Saturday nights were standing dates with Michelle and whether we went to the football game or not, I'd have to be back to take her out or we really would break up. When you're going with a girl, Saturday night dates are just part of the package.

I was really psyched up about going to see Sandy run on Saturday, so psyched up in fact that in our own meet on Friday night I won both the mile and the 5,000 meter. I didn't break any records or anything, but I turned out to be one of the stars that night. My parents and Chrissie were there to see me and so was Michelle with some of her friends. They were all really excited for me and all the congratulations I was getting were going to my head. I also knew there were scouts from some of the colleges at the meet and since I was hoping to get a track scholarship I was really feeling good.

Kenny brought me back to earth on the bus going back after the meet by saying to me, "Lucky for us that little girl isn't on our team or we wouldn't be getting so much attention."

Kenny had won his event, too, but then he usually did.

Zabo's voice spoke up from behind us and I realized that he'd overheard what Kenny said.

"Maybe lucky for you guys, but I'd sure like her on the team."

I turned around, eager for any talk about Sandy. "Did you try to get her, Zabo?"

He chuckled. "You don't know how I tried. What did I have to offer her, though, Palos Verdes? She's going to be competing in New York, Europe—you name it. I guess I'm just going to have to be happy with you guys."

Then the coach started in on a little replay of what had happened that night and I sort of tuned him out and began thinking about seeing Sandy run the following day. I was making up all sorts of conversations in my mind that I could have with her if we got a chance to speak to each other, and of course in every single conversation I came across sounding a whole lot better than I'd managed to sound in person when we actually had spoken. But that's the way it always is.

When I left Kenny, I told him I'd pick him up about nine the next morning, then I went on home where my folks and Chrissie were waiting up for me. My dad and I talked about the track meet and Chrissie piped in once in a while describing which guys on the team she thought were the best-looking, then my mom made us some popcorn to have before we went to bed. I didn't call Michelle as I usually did before I went to bed, but for all I knew she was still out with her friends.

I was so excited it was hard to get to sleep. It was like when I was a little kid on the night before Christmas. I woke up earlier than I usually did on a weekend too. I took a shower and washed my hair and then got dressed in Levi's and a T-shirt. It was hot that day, but I decided to wear my school jacket in red and gold so that maybe Sandy would see me at the meet. I know how stupid this all sounds—I wasn't acting cool at all—but I just couldn't seem to help it.

It was a long, boring drive down to San Diego and then when we finally found the Sports Arena we learned that the meet wasn't during the day at all, it was at night.

Kenny wasn't too pleased with me by that time. First, I'd been lost in thought during the drive and wasn't much of a conversationalist, then I got us down there about eight hours too early.

I thought he was going to insist we turn right around and drive back to Long Beach so I suggested that we spend the day at the beach. Kenny had it in his head, though, that he wanted to see the San Diego Zoo, and since I wanted to keep him happy, that's where we went. It's a really great zoo and Kenny enjoyed it and I probably would have too if my mind hadn't been on seeing Sandy run that night.

I'm not going to bore you with the details of the whole track meet. We didn't get very good seats and as it turned out we were lucky to get seats at all because the meet was practically sold out. And a lot of that was due to all the advance publicity Sandy had received in the San Diego papers. I didn't hear about that stuff until later, though.

I enjoyed watching the meet because I'm really into track, but from the program I could see that the first event she was running was the 880 and I was really waiting for that to begin.

By the time her event was called you could sense the ripple of anticipation from the audience and I could even hear people around us saying her name. I had honestly thought I was the only one down there to watch her, but it turned out that she was the feature attraction.

All the athletes limbering up on the sidelines stopped to watch the race and some of the top names in the track world took up positions for a good view. Everyone applauded politely when the names of the other entrants were given, but when Sandy's name was called and she ran a few steps forward to acknowledge it, the cheers were deafening, and I found myself standing up and screaming my head off.

When the gun went off to start the race, she took charge almost immediately, forging to the front and building up her lead with each circle of the track. The other girls tried to match her pace, but they never had a chance. After two lapses she was a few yards ahead, and after four, more than ten yards. From then on it was only a question of how good a time she would set. She had already won it hands down.

As she blazed past the line at the halfway point the announcer's voice boomed out the figures and the crowd erupted even louder as they realized she was on her way to breaking a record.

I could see a faint smile on her face as she increased her speed a bit, lapped one runner and drew close to another. At the six-lap mark she was still ahead of the record and the crowd clamored for more.

Around the oval she sped as the gun lap came up and, showing no signs of being tired, she responded to the crack of the pistol with another burst of speed. Kenny was just as excited watching it as I was, and by this point he was pounding me on the back and yelling.

A few seconds later, she was past the far straight and into the final turn as officials with sensing devices and hand-held instruments monitored her progress into the final ten yards. Seven yards from the tape, her time was noted for the 800-meter distance as she streaked for the finish line. In a blur of motion she hit the tape and slowed down to take a victory lap before the wildly cheering crowd.

I could hear people around me saying that she had probably set a new record. As I waited for the announcer's voice I watched her as she wiped the sweat off her face and accepted congratulations from her teammates. Finally it came. For the 880 yards, the loudspeaker booms, 2:01.4, a new world's record. And the time for 800 meters was 2:01.8, also the fastest ever recorded for a woman. And by a girl! A fourteen-year-old girl!

I should have realized right then that she wasn't in my league. I might be a senior and popular and all, and not too bad at track, either, but this kid was a phenomenon and she was just starting out.

"I'm sure glad I got to see this," said Kenny, finally sitting down and catching his breath. "Have you ever seen anything more awesome than the way that little girl ran?"

"Never," I agreed.

"Well, I'm about to show you something more awesome."

I looked over at him.

"I'm about to consume eight hot dogs in a row; you want to come out with me?"

I checked the program and saw that Sandy wasn't running again for a while, so we went out and filled up on hot dogs and Cokes, then went back in to watch the rest of the events.

She won the mile, of course, but it was nowhere near as exciting as the 880 had been, mostly because she didn't have any competition at all and just ran away with it. She also didn't break the record, but she came very close.

My idea of getting close enough to talk to her afterward was an impossibility. For one thing, she was surrounded by TV cameras and reporters, and for another, I had the feeling she wouldn't even recognize me if I did say something to her.

We were halfway home when I remembered about my date with Michelle.

"You're in trouble now," said Kenny when I mentioned it to him.

"What's the worst she can do to me?"

"Break up."

"Yeah." That's exactly what I'd been thinking. And if I were a nice guy I'd let her break up with me because at the moment she'd be a lot better off without me. Plenty of guys would want to take her out, and any of them would give her a lot more time and attention than I'd been giving her lately.

And I knew what was keeping me from ending it with Michelle was a feeling that there was no way I was going to get anywhere with Sandy. I hated to think I was that self-ish, but I guess I was. If Sandy had shown any interest in me whatsoever there was no doubt in my mind that Michelle would get left behind. But Sandy didn't even know I was alive. If she flirted with boys I hadn't had any indication of it, and for that matter maybe she wasn't even interested in boys yet. She was fourteen, sure, but she looked younger and could very well be slow in that respect.

"You're a fool if you let Michelle get away." Kenny didn't often give advice, but when he did it was usually sound.

"I know that," I told him, "but on the other hand..."

"On the other hand you're interested in that little girl."

"Quit referring to her as 'that little girl,' Kenny. Call her Sandy."

"She doesn't even look old enough to date."

"She's fourteen."

"Tell me the truth, Tom, would you be at all interested in her if she didn't run so well?"

"I wouldn't have even noticed her."

"That's what I mean. She doesn't appeal to you as a girl, she just appeals to you as a runner. Hey, she appeals to all of us that way. Don't you think the whole team is impressed by her? It would be impossible not to be."

"Look, Kenny, your girlfriend is on the track team—you two have something in common."

"You think we spend our time talking about track? I get that with you; I don't need it with a girl."

I tried to imagine dancing with Sandy or kissing her, but I couldn't get the picture clear in my mind. I could imagine running with her, but then that's all I'd ever seen her do.

And naturally, imagining running with her was imagining being beaten by her.

"It doesn't seem fair to hang on to Michelle while I spend all my time thinking about Sandy."

"Since when are boy-girl relationships ever fair?"

"I've always tried to be."

"Yeah, I know you have. My advice to you is to forget Sandy. Think of her like the girls think of rock stars— someone to admire, but from a distance."

"It has been from a distance. I don't even know where she lives and there're about a million Smiths in the phone book."

"She lives in Naples."

When he said that, I turned to him so fast I almost lost control of the car. Kenny reached over, righted the wheel, and told me to take it easy.

"How do you know where she lives?"

"Billie told me."

Billie is his girlfriend. "How does Billie know?"

"We were talking about her one day and Billie said she lived down the street from her."

"What else did she tell you?"

"I don't know—that was a while back."

"Try to remember, okay?"

Kenny gave me a downtrodden look. "Maybe if you were to pull off the freeway into that McDonald's I see up ahead my memory would return to me."

I was so late getting home anyway a few more minutes wouldn't matter. I pulled into the parking lot of the Mc-Donald's and we both went inside.

"All right," I said to him when he'd demolished one burger and was starting in on his second, "tell me what you know."

"Not a whole lot."

"Kenny!"

"All right, all right, just let me finish this, okay?" He began chomping at his second burger while I watched him in silence. I couldn't believe he hadn't told me any of this before, knowing, as he did, how interested I was.

Kenny finally finished chewing and took a long sip of his milkshake. "Listen, Tom, I don't know much."

"Just tell me what you know."

"Well, she's an only child and lives with her mother, who's divorced."

He paused while I digested that bit of information. I wasn't about to make her out as some poor half-orphan because half the kids I knew had divorced parents. "Go on," I finally said when it seemed as though Kenny had nothing more to say.

"She was always a quiet, skinny little kid who kept to herself and who didn't have any friends in the neighborhood."

It didn't sound as though she had changed much. "And?" I prompted him.

"No one knew she could run until they had what they call Field Days when she was in junior high. Seems she outran everyone in every track event. One of the gym teachers got pretty excited about her and I guess he's the one who put the coach over at Runners West onto her."

"What else?"

"I think that was all. Listen, Tom, Billie and I had other things to do, you know?" He winked at me conspiratorily but I wasn't amused.

"But you could find out more, couldn't you?"

He shrugged lazily, a big grin on his face. "If you're really interested."

That succeeded in getting a laugh out of me. Even I could see I was getting too serious about a girl I didn't even know.

And yet that was part of her appeal to me, the fact that she was a mystery and one I was interested in solving.

I didn't take him straight home that night but made him show me where Sandy lived first. Naples is a little town bordering on Belmont Shore, and the reason it's called Naples is because it has all these canals winding through it. Most of the houses are tiny with hardly any property around them at all, but there are a few larger ones directly on the canals where people keep their boats out in front of their houses.

Sandy's house wasn't on a canal and was very small and nondescript, looking like not much more than a playhouse. I saw the car I had followed parked in front and there was a light on inside, but it was late and the street was deserted.

I checked it out quickly and then pulled away, not wanting Kenny to know how excited I was. If he hadn't been along I swear I probably would have sat there all night. At least I now knew where she lived and maybe I could get Kenny to invite me over to Billie's house, where I might accidentally run into Sandy out in front.

It gave me a lot to think about, anyway.

Michelle and I didn't exactly break up over my missing our date but it amounted to the same thing. And it makes me sad now to think that at the time I felt good about it.

I got up early the next morning and rushed downstairs to get the paper. There was a picture, on page one this time, of Sandy crossing the finish line, and also an article devoted exclusively to her. It didn't say anything personal about her except her age and where she was from, but it did list the places where she'd be running in the next few months. A couple of them I'd be able to go to, but the rest were too far away.

I knew I was really hooked when the phone rang and it was Michelle and I hadn't even thought about calling her first. She sounded serious and a little sad and asked if I'd come by and talk to her.

"Listen, Michelle, about last night—"

"I'd rather talk to you in person, Tom," she said, and something about her voice then made me think she'd been crying. I told her I'd be over as soon as I put some clothes on.

Michelle's parents are really nice and her mom asked me if I wanted to eat breakfast with them when I got there. I said sure, partly because I was starved and she had made pancakes, and partly because I could prolong the time before I'd have to talk to Michelle alone.

I can remember exactly what she was wearing that morning and she looked really pretty. She was wearing jeans and a light blue cashmere sweater with a V neck, and around her neck she was wearing the silver heart I'd given her for Christmas. She even had lipstick on and had outlined her eyes. I thought she was probably the prettiest girl I'd ever seen.

I'm ashamed to say I had two helpings of pancakes and dragged out my eating time so that I was there a good half hour before Michelle and I went out on her patio to talk. She sat down on the glider where we usually sat together and I took a seat in one of the chairs. It was a sunny, warm morning and her dog was running around the yard and everything was perfectly normal except the look in Michelle's eyes.

"I'm really sorry about last night, Michelle," I began, but she cut in on me.

"Are you?"

"Sure I am."

"Couldn't you have called at least?"

Of course I could have and she knew it as well as I did. I tried to look contrite but she was gazing over my head and didn't even notice.

"Where were you, Tom?"

"Kenny and I went down to San Diego to a track meet."

She was nodding as though she'd already known, but I don't think she could have as I hadn't told anybody.

"Things aren't good between us anymore, Tom, and I honestly don't think it's my fault."

"Oh, I don't know—"

"Let's not play games, Tom; let's be honest with each other, okay?"

I could see she was close to tears so I nodded in agreement. Anyway, she was right.

"I think it might be a good idea if we didn't see each other for a while. I'm not being vindictive, Tom. I'm not breaking up with you because you stood me up last night. I've given it a lot of thought and...and..."

At that point she started crying and I felt so bad I could've cried myself. I had liked that girl so much, had been so close to her, and now I was ruining it for no good reason at all. And yet I didn't rush to her side and comfort her as I should have done. I just sat there and felt relief that it was all being taken out of my hands. She was doing the breaking up so I figured that I must be the innocent party.

"Is this like a trial separation?" I asked, my tone sounding flippant even to my own ears.

She nodded, the tears streaming down her face. "I thought we could try it for a month, see how it goes."

"Are you going to go out with other guys?" I had to ask. I had to see if I was completely free to pursue Sandy.

"I don't know—I haven't thought about that yet. But I want you to feel free to do as you please."

So that was that, I actually had her okay. I was sitting there wondering how soon I could leave and maybe cruise by Sandy's house when she got up and ran into the house.

It was a little embarrassing saying goodbye to her folks after they had seen her run by crying, but as I said, they're nice people and they made it easy on me. They probably just thought it was a misunderstanding that would soon be cleared up. It wasn't as though Michelle and I hadn't fought before.

I must have driven by Sandy's house a hundred and fifty times that day, but I didn't see her even once.

That night I cut Sandy's picture out of the paper and also the article and took them up to my room. I was removing Michelle's picture from my corkboard and putting Sandy's in her place when Chrissie walked unannounced into my room.

I was certainly not going to be so juvenile as to hide what I was doing from my sister, but if boys can blush that's what I was doing.

"Who's that, Tommy?" she asked me, walking over for a closer look.

"A runner," I mumbled.

"Why're you taking Michelle's picture down?"

"We split up."

She took a long time looking from Michelle's picture to Sandy's and then shook her head in disgust. "You broke up with Michelle for *her*?"

"She's a great runner, Chrissie."

"But look at her—she doesn't look like anything. If I looked like that none of the boys would even call me up."

"Looks aren't that important," I told her, forgetting for a moment that I had always judged girls solely by their looks.

"Boys think they are," she said, and I couldn't really argue with that.

"Anyway, I didn't break up with Michelle for her. Michelle broke up with me, and I just admire this girl as a runner, that's all. I don't even know her."

"How old is she?"

"Fourteen."

I figured she'd have something to say about our age differences, but all she said was, "That's pretty young to have her picture in the paper."

"She's getting pretty famous," I told her.

"Do I get to meet her?"

"Maybe one of these days, I don't know."

"I liked Michelle."

"Look, I still like Michelle, we just weren't getting along, that's all."

"Yeah, I know what you mean. Bobby Carruthers made me kiss him at the party and I can't stand him now."

I had to laugh at that. "You're a little young for kissing, aren't you?"

"That's what I told him, but he wouldn't listen."

"Well, next time punch him in the mouth."

She grinned at me. "I did."

I figured Chrissie was going to be all right. About myself, I wasn't so sure.

Chapter Three

It was mid-November before I began to make any progress in getting to know Sandy. Cruising by her house had proved to be fruitless—she was either never at home or never sitting outside. A couple of times I tried saying something to her during practice, but she always answered in monosyllables, leaving me feeling more frustrated than ever.

Then one day I hit upon a fantastic idea and wondered why I hadn't thought of it sooner.

I was driving Kenny home after practice and I said, real casually, "Want to drive by Runners West for a few minutes?"

He laughed out loud. "How long have you had this one up your sleeve?"

I gave a sheepish grin. "I just thought of it today."

"Yeah, I don't mind. I'd like to see some of the competition I'm going to run into later on."

Kenny had already been offered a full track scholarship to Oregon and he was going to take it. I'd been tentatively approached by them, but also by UCLA, and it was my first choice. Track was a lot of fun, but I eventually wanted to be a doctor and UCLA had a good med school. Kenny kept trying to get me to change my mind, but while I would have enjoyed going to the same college as him, I was pretty serious about my future. Also, UCLA was much closer to home.

I was on the Garden Grove Freeway before Kenny said, "You getting anyplace with her?"

I shook my head. "She barely talks to me even if I force it."

"Billie says she's shy."

"She's not shy on the track."

"Yeah, but that's different."

"She doesn't seem interested, but if I could just get to know her..."

"Maybe I could arrange something."

"Like what?"

He shrugged. "I don't know, maybe Billie could have a party or something and invite her."

"Do you think she would?" I was sure I could get her interested in me in a party situation. That was my kind of turf and she'd be new to it.

"If I asked her real nice."

"Would you?"

He punched me in the arm. "I just might do that for my buddy. I'd sure like to do something to cheer you up. You're a real grouch lately, you know that?"

"I haven't been that bad, have I?"

"I make allowances since you're obviously in love."

That hit me harder than the punch in the arm. "How can I be in love? I don't even know her."

"That's the worst kind. If you knew her you'd probably get back to normal, but since it's all fantasy..."

I think he was right about that, it was all the mystery surrounding her that was driving me crazy. Maybe if I actually got to know her she'd bore me to death. I didn't want that to be the case, though. I had to feel this would come to something or I would've split with Michelle for no reason.

Runners West turned out to have a nice facility and a good cinder track. The guy in charge let us look through the building that housed locker-room facilities as well as a weight room with a lot of Nautilus equipment. I lifted weights over at Kenny's house just once in a while, but if I had a place like this to work out at I'd probably really get into it.

We went out the rear door onto the field where the track was, and there was Sandy and a bunch of others running while the coach stood by timing them.

When we walked over to him he looked up from the stopwatch and gave us a big smile. "Well, well. Tom Cunningham and Kenny Allen, I'm honored. You come by to join up?"

I was really surprised he knew who we were. He must have known this because he said, "I've checked you out a few times, made inquiries. Saw you at Palos Verdes not long ago."

"I figured you'd only be interested in the big names," Kenny said to him.

"Never know who's going to be big—you two have the potential. Zabo's real big on you boys. What are you planning on doing after high school?"

Kenny and I looked at each other. "He's going to Oregon and I'm hoping for UCLA," I told him.

"Not bad choices, not bad at all. Sure I can't tempt you to give up college and join me?"

Kenny was looking pretty interested and I knew he hated the thought of four more years of school, but I also knew his parents, like mine, were dead set on his getting a college education.

"I'm planning on being a doctor," I said.

"What about you?" he asked Kenny.

"I guess I'll end up a coach," he said, but didn't sound happy about it.

Coach Jenkins laughed. "Well, there're worse things to end up as."

"I didn't mean—" began Kenny.

"I know you didn't. But if either of you boys should change your mind, you know where I am. I understand Sandy works out with you guys after school."

"Not exactly *with* us," I said, and he laughed.

"She's something else, isn't she? Hey, Sandy," he yelled, "come on over here."

I tried to look very cool as Sandy came off the track and trotted up to us.

"A couple of classmates of yours are here," the coach was saying. "I made 'em an offer but it was no dice."

"You trying to bribe them?" she asked him. It was the first time I'd ever heard her talk naturally with someone, and then she smiled at the coach and I was enchanted. Dumb word, enchanted, but that's the only way to describe it. Her whole face lit up and she looked almost pretty, and I could see that if she made an effort at it she really could be pretty.

"Would I do that?" he teased her, putting an arm around her shoulders. "Do you know these guys or should I introduce you?"

She looked over at us. "I know them. I've never spoken to Kenny, but I've watched him work out."

Kenny's smile was splitting his face. "We saw you down in San Diego and I've got only one word to describe it. Awesome!"

She looked over at me and then back at Kenny. "You were down there?"

"We wanted to see if you were as good as we'd heard," he told her, and I could see she was pleased.

The coach put his hands on her shoulders and pointed her in the direction of the track. "Back to work, young lady."

She gave us each a smile before she headed back and for the very first time I felt I was making some progress with her. True, she hadn't actually spoken to me, but she had smiled, and that had to mean something, didn't it?

We stuck around for a while talking to the coach. He questioned us about our training and even sneaked in some advice, trying all the while not to sound as though he were invading Zabo's territory. He seemed to think neither of us were pushing ourselves to our limits, and he was probably right about that. Zabo was a good coach but he wasn't really tough.

When we left he told us to come back anytime and feel free to work out with his people if we wanted. I didn't know whether Kenny was interested, but I sure was.

"Nice guy" was Kenny's only comment as we got into the car.

"Nice setup," I answered.

"Yeah, I wouldn't mind working out over there once in a while. Did you get a look at that Nautilus equipment?"

I nodded.

"You're not fooling me one bit with that cool act of yours, Tom. If I said the word you'd be over there every day, am I right?"

I grinned. "She smiled at me."

"She smiled at both of us."

"Yeah, but I felt it was all for me."

He chuckled. "I'll let you get away with that one but only because I can't stand to see a guy cry."

I was thankful to have Kenny as a friend. I knew I wouldn't have had the guts to have gone to the meet or over to Runners West on my own. He was a good buddy, all right.

We came to a compromise about when we'd work out with the athletes at Runners West. I was all for going over there every day and Kenny was all for going over there once in a while, so we compromised on Tuesdays and Thursdays after practice.

It seemed as though once I got one good idea I seemed to get more. We practiced with Runners West for a couple of weeks and Sandy got used to seeing us there and even opened up so far as to say hello to us a couple of times. Then one day after practice at school I waylaid her on the way to the gym.

"Listen," I said to her, "why don't we give you a ride over to Runners West on Tuesdays and Thursdays? We can give you a ride home, too, and your mom would get a little time off."

She seemed to be thinking about it. "Okay, I'll ask her," she finally said. "That way she wouldn't have to take time off work so much."

When I told Kenny the new plan, he said, "I was wondering when you were going to think of that." Kenny likes me to think he's always one step ahead of me even when he isn't.

That day, when Sandy's mom picked her up, I watched as she motioned for her mother to come over to the track. I figured Sandy was going to put my plan to her, and since I know how fussy girls' parents are about what boys they hang around, I gave them a little time and then walked over, determined to make a good impression.

When I got up close to them I didn't say anything at first—her mother was such a surprise. She was small like Sandy, only she looked like a woman and not a little girl. She had long hair parted in the middle, just like most of the high-school girls wear it, and if I hadn't known it was Sandy's mother I would have thought she was a college student. I did some mental calculation in my head and figured she had to be in her thirties, but she sure didn't look it.

Sandy introduced us and her mother gave me the kind of look and smile I'd hoped to get one day from Sandy. I would have sworn she was flirting with me, only I'd never had someone's mother flirt with me before.

"Sandy tells me you've offered to drive her here and home on Tuesdays and Thursdays," she said, holding out her hand for me to shake.

I made a production of wiping my sweaty hands off on my pants and by that time she'd dropped her hand and half her smile.

I shrugged. "Since we're coming over here anyway..."

"I'd appreciate it," she told me, making very strong eye contact. "I sell real estate and it's not always convenient to get over here."

I was so elated by the news I almost offered to drive Sandy home every day, but some small voice inside me cautioned me not to push my luck.

Now all I had was five days to wait in order to give Sandy her first ride.

So Sandy began meeting us at my car on Tuesdays and Thursdays after practice, just naturally getting into the back seat and leaving the front seat to us. Of course I would have preferred having her ride up front beside me, but there was no point in rushing things and scaring her off. Because I had an idea she would be scared off easily.

On the drive over to Garden Grove, and also on the ride back to her house, as long as the conversation revolved around track, Sandy would chime in once in a while with some remark or other. But if Kenny and I started talking about anything else, like what movies we'd seen or some song that was playing on the radio, or anything at all for that matter, Sandy would just sit silently in the back seat. From what I could see of her face in the rearview mirror, she wasn't listening to us at all but just thinking her own thoughts.

I began to find out that it was even more frustrating to have her in the car with me and not be able to get any closer to her than I would if she had not been there. Kenny, good friend that he was, made an excuse not to go along with us one Thursday, telling me he had a doctor's appointment.

"You're going to the doctor?" I asked him. "What's the matter with you?"

"Nothing's the matter with me, it's just my yearly checkup, that's all."

"I think you're making that up so I can be alone with Sandy. You don't have to do that, you know."

"Listen, I'm not making anything up. You know how my mom is about doctors. She can hardly wait until you're one so she can save some money."

I was still dubious about whether or not he had a doctor's appointment, but I didn't give him much of an argument because it was going to be my first chance to be alone with Sandy.

I was as nervous as a kid on his first date when Sandy showed up and I told her she could sit in the front seat. I only hoped I wouldn't blow the opportunity.

"Where's Kenny?" she asked, getting in and closing the door.

"He had a doctor's appointment."

She didn't seem to find anything strange in that and lapsed into her usual silence. I kept stealing glances at her as I drove but as far as I could see she never looked at me once, just stared out the window as though she were monitoring my driving.

It was two miles before I thought of something to say, and then it was just whether she was enjoying Wilson High.

"It's okay," she said, her voice expressionless.

"Do you ever go to any of the games?" I asked her.

"Games?"

She made me feel like I was speaking a foreign language. "Yeah, you know, any of the football games."

She shook her head and mumbled something.

"What?"

"I don't understand football," she said.

"That doesn't matter, none of the girls do. It's still fun to go."

She didn't say anything to that so I didn't follow up by asking her to a football game. "Do you see any movies?" I was sure this was something everyone understood.

"I used to, with my mother, but she's dating this guy now...."

I began to feel sorry for her. There had to be something in her life besides running, and I wanted to find out what it was.

"What shows do you like on TV?"

"We don't have a TV."

I had never even heard of anyone not having a TV. Talk about deprived homes!

I was getting nowhere fast with my attempts at conversation but we were in Garden Grove by then anyway. The entire time I worked out I kept trying to think of what to say to her on the way home. If I didn't say anything, it was obvious that she wasn't going to.

On the way home I asked her if she wanted to stop at a Burger King and get something to eat.

"I don't want anything, but I don't mind stopping for you," she said politely.

I decided to take her up on it since it'd give me more time alone with her and this was my big chance.

I went into Burger King and brought back two hamburgers and a Coke to the car. I figured if she'd changed her mind she could have one of them and we'd share the drink.

"Sure you don't want some?" I asked her, feeling kind of greedy eating all by myself.

"I'm a vegetarian."

"You don't think animals should be killed, huh?"

She looked over at me, her eyes a clear gray. "I don't have any feelings about cows," she said. "I don't eat meat because it's not healthy."

"Not even a rare steak?" I asked.

She shook her head.

I offered her a drink of my Coke but she declined. "I've eliminated sugar from my diet, too."

Well I knew she was right about Cokes not being good for you, but I figured if you eliminated sugar from your diet you'd be eliminating just about anything that was good to eat.

"So I guess you're a health-food freak," I said, joking with her.

"I just don't want to rely on false energy when I'm running," she told me seriously.

"Does your coach approve of your diet?"

She nodded. "He's very big on diet. I think most of his runners eat about the same as I do."

I was so desperate by then to have something to talk to her about, to have something in common besides running, that I found myself asking her if she could write out her diet for me. "If it would help my running I'd be willing to give it a try," I told her.

She gave kind of a half-smile and I figured I'd finally hit upon something that interested her. "I'll write it out for you tonight," she told me.

"Look, do you ever do anything besides run?" I asked her on the way to her house. If she said no I was out of luck, but if she said yes maybe we'd have something else to talk about. I'd never met a girl who talked so little, usually they monopolize a conversation.

"What do you mean?"

"I mean is that all you do? All you think about?"

"It takes up most of my time, if that's what you mean."

"What do you do for fun?"

She looked confused. "I think running's fun."

Really stretching, I asked, "What do you want to be when you grow up?" If she said a runner, the heck with it.

She merely said, "I'm only fourteen," and that really shut me up. There was no reason for her to be thinking about what she wanted to be when she grew up since she had hardly even started to grow.

When we got to her house, I shut off the engine and was going to make one last attempt at some conversation, but she said a quick thank-you and got right out of the car.

True to her promise, the next day Sandy handed me a piece of notebook paper after school, and when I opened it up it was the diet she'd promised me. To tell the truth I'd forgotten all about it by then and thought she had written me a letter, but no such luck.

That night after dinner (I figured I was entitled to one last meal) I gave my mom the diet and told her that was how I wanted to eat from now on.

She read it through quickly and started to laugh. "Are you serious, Tom?"

"I've decided to get healthy," I told her.

"But there's hardly anything on here you like. It's easy enough if that's what you want; it doesn't take any culinary ability to give you a plate of raw vegetables."

"I'd like to stick to it if you don't mind," I told her.

"I don't mind, I just hope you don't starve to death."

That weekend I ate nothing but eggs and fruit and raw vegetables and drank lots of milk, and the healthy combination managed to give me a very upset stomach. But my mother said it was just that my system was cleansing itself and not to worry about it.

It was horrible, though, never having one thing to eat that I really liked. At the football game on Saturday night I had to look away whenever I saw someone eating a hot dog, because if I didn't I was afraid I'd snatch it right out of the person's hands.

I was beginning to hate Saturday nights. I had always spent my Saturday nights either with Michelle alone or going to a party, but now I couldn't do either. I knew that Michelle would probably be at the parties and I didn't feel like seeing her socially just yet. And Kenny and the other guys all dated their girlfriends Saturday nights.

The alternative was staying home and watching TV with my folks, and that didn't appeal to me, either. So I took to parking outside Sandy's house on Saturday nights and trying not to wear down my car battery by leaving the radio on.

I never saw her. A couple of times I saw her mother leaving on a date, but if Sandy was home she never even looked out the front window. I was lonely and now I was getting hungry all the time, but I still felt all it would take was some time before Sandy and I became friends.

Around the end of November, one of my friends, Gary Rowe, stopped me after school one day and asked me if I was still going with Michelle.

"We've kind of split up," I told him.

"No kidding?"

I shrugged.

"What I wanted to ask you, Tom, would you mind if I asked her out?"

I felt a little angry at first since Gary and I had double-dated frequently when I'd been going with Michelle, and I was wondering now if he'd wanted to be with her all that time. Then I told myself I had no right to feel angry, that Michelle didn't belong to me anymore.

"Go right ahead," I told him, "she's a free agent."

"You're sure you wouldn't mind?"

"No, as a matter of fact I know she always liked you."

"I feel like I'm trying to steal your girlfriend."

In a magnanimous gesture, I put my arm around his shoulders and walked outside the school with him. "Listen, what can I tell you? I think it'd be great if you two got together."

"Who're you dating now?" he asked me, a question I got asked quite frequently lately.

"At the moment I'm just concentrating on my running."

He looked mystified at that, as well he should. "You've given up girls?"

I made an effort to look enigmatic. "Not quite."

He didn't push it further, grateful, I guess, that I'd given him the okay on Michelle.

What I hadn't counted on was Michelle.

Up until then we'd been pretty much ignoring each other around school, but a few days after talking to Gary she cornered me in the hall, her face furious.

"Where do you get off giving people *permission* to date me, Tom Cunningham?"

She looked so pretty standing there in her red sweater with her eyes blazing that I had to smile. "What're you talking about?"

"You know very well what I'm talking about! I'm talking about Gary! I'll have you know I don't need your help in getting dates. I also don't need your permission!"

"Hey, Michelle," I started to say, but she'd already run off and left me standing there.

Up until then I don't think Michelle had dated anyone else because I would have been sure to hear about it if she had. But not long after that encounter I started seeing her all over school with Mike Stern, and that was a shock.

I got along with Mike all right, but he wasn't the kind of guy I'd want to see my sister date. He had a reputation for drinking a lot and driving recklessly and coming on far too strong with the girls. He could rarely get one of the nice girls in the school to go out with him, but while they were afraid of him, they also all found him sexy. Which is a dangerous combination, I guess.

For a while I felt kind of guilty, like I had thrown Michelle to the lions, but then I told myself that she was sixteen and ought to know what she was doing by then. Mike had to be her choice because I was sure she could get any number of guys if she wanted. It still bothered me to see her with him, though, and I found myself not talking to him much anymore.

After I got used to it I found I was feeling pretty good on my new diet and I tried to interest Kenny in it. He said if I ever got as fast as Sandy he might give it a try, but until then he'd stick to good old regular food. Which made it hard on me because I had to watch him eat all that good old regular food.

Sandy and I at least had something to talk about now besides track. She'd ask me how my diet was going, and I'd tell her fine and maybe ask her a question or two about different foods.

But I knew I wasn't really getting anywhere with her and I knew I'd have to come up with another good idea soon.

Chapter Four

The first weekend in December Sandy appeared at an indoor track meet up in L.A., and I talked Kenny into going only on the condition that Billie could come along too. She'd known Sandy since she was a little kid and was just as interested in track as we were, so I readily agreed. Also, Billie didn't like it much when I messed up her Saturday night dates with Kenny.

Kenny drove since my Mustang had developed some engine trouble and for once his car was in working condition. This meant I had to sit in the back seat while he and Billie sat in the front, which I don't suppose sounds like any big deal except that I get very nervous sitting in the back seat of a car. If I'm not driving myself, I at least like to be in the front where I can supervise the driving when I think it's called for.

Billie is really pretty and the only black girl I know who has green eyes, rather like a cat. She kind of half liked me and half resented me. I know she liked me as a person because we always got along fine, but she resented the fact that Kenny and I spent so much time together. But some girls are like that, they want to monopolize you and don't understand that sometimes boys need to be together and talk about things girls aren't interested in. Although that hadn't been the case lately: Billie was just as interested in talking about track as we were, and most of the time we'd been talking about girls, or to be more specific—Sandy.

I was wearing a new white turtleneck sweater my mom had bought to try to get me out of my sweatshirts once in a while. I was hoping it would make me stand out in the crowd enough so that Sandy would see me, but that was before we got up there and I saw how many thousands of people had come. You would have thought it was the World Series or something, there were so many people.

Kenny, in a gesture I considered sadistic, bought hot dogs and Cokes for himself and Billie before we found our seats, and I had to sit there and smell those good smells and listen to them eat, all the while suffering in silence. I guess it was like when my dad gave up smoking a couple of years ago and kept craving cigarettes for the longest time. I was feeling really good on my new diet, but I still got visions in my head of hot dogs and hamburgers and pizza and tacos and about a thousand other things I could name.

There was a pole vaulter from the East there that night who got a lot of attention. He held the record but he was out to break his own record, and he did, and flashbulbs were going off all over the place. Kenny and I were yelling and cheering and Billie was grumbling that there weren't any women pole vaulters, and then the announcement was made for the girls' 880 and I stopped paying attention to anything but Sandy's slight figure coming out on the track, looking about two inches tall from where I was sitting.

There was a ringing ovation when her name was announced and I tried to control myself so that Billie wouldn't get the wrong idea. Or I guess I mean the right idea. Kenny gave me a knowing look before settling back to watch the race.

When the gun went off, Sandy worked her way to the front by the end of the first lap around the wooden oval and stayed there as some of the best runners in the Amateur Athletic Union's ranks fought to stay close. As I watched, she steadily widened the gap between her flying feet and that of the next runner. She ran without obvious strain, so fluidly it was hard to believe she was going exceptionally fast. But as the announcer reported the lap times, it was obvious she was setting a blistering pace.

I swear I was so tense my muscles were knotting as I loudly cheered her on. At the halfway point she was twenty or thirty yards in front and the crowd was picking up the tempo of its cheering as though encouraging her to break a record. She continued to flash over the dark green track divided into narrow lanes by a series of white lines.

At the three-quarter mark, she was still ahead of the record. The crowd raised its volume still more and she seemed to respond with more effort. Finally the last lap came up. The starter raised his gun as Sandy came out of the banked turn and down the home straightaway. The report of the blank shell indicated the "gun" lap reverberated through the arena as she swept into the last hundred yards.

Sure-footedly she made her way across the final stretch with no one closer than half a lap to her darting form. The officials stretched the white tape across the finish line as she rounded the last turn and headed for home. Split seconds later she hit the tape, dragging the thin white cord with her as the approval of the crowd reached a crescendo. When the officials completed checking the time, an expectant hush fell over the audience. The deep voice came over the loud-speaker. "In the women's 880-yard run, first place, Sandy Smith, in 2:00.7—a new world's record!"

I was screaming my head off at that and Kenny was pounding my back and screaming along with me. I looked over at Billie and saw that tears were streaming down her face; she was as moved by it as we were.

I was so proud of her I could've burst, and I was also a little jealous. I knew I'd never be that good in a million years and I began to think it was a good thing I wanted to be a doctor, because if my whole life revolved around track, like hers seemed to, I'd be plain out of luck.

On the drive back to Long Beach, Kenny asked Billie what she'd think of having a party at her place some Saturday night.

Billie turned around in the front seat and gave me an amused look. "And I don't happen to suppose you'd want me to invite Sandy, now would you?" she asked me, and I could hear Kenny's chuckle in response.

"Well, she is a neighbor of yours, isn't she?" I asked her, all innocence.

"I'm not at all sure she'd come," said Billie, "she's not very sociable."

"But you know her, don't you?"

"Sure I know her, she's a neighbor."

Then Kenny had a brilliant idea. "Tell her it's a party for the track team, why don't you? Maybe if she thinks we're going to be running around instead of dancing, it will appeal to her."

"You shouldn't be encouraging him in this," Billie said with a sigh. "Sandy's not interested in boys."

"Then it's about time she started to be," retorted Kenny, and I silently applauded him.

"Okay," said Billie. "I'll have a party next Saturday night, and I'll invite Sandy, but I can't promise she'll come."

I knew Sandy didn't have a meet scheduled for the following Saturday and I was sure she was the kind of person to be too polite to turn down an invitation from a neighbor. At least I was hoping that was the case.

That week I walked around in a state of euphoria. Billie had asked her to the party on Tuesday, and Sandy had said she would come. I didn't even bring up the subject of the party when we drove her to practice on Tuesday in case she might change her mind, but on Thursday she brought it up herself.

"You're going with Billie Harmon, aren't you, Kenny?" she asked him.

"That's right," he told her.

"Then you'll be at the party Saturday night?"

Kenny glanced over at me. "We both will."

I was watching her in the rearview mirror and I could sense she was trying to get up her courage to ask something else. Then I saw Kenny turn around in the seat and I guess he realized the same thing, 'cause he said to her, "Your first high-school party?"

She nodded.

"Listen," he told her, "it's nothing to be nervous about. It'll just be a bunch of kids, mostly the track team. We'll have some food, listen to some music.... Tell me something, Sandy, do you get nervous at those big meets?"

"I did at first," she said.

"Well, if you can ace those, you won't have any trouble at the party. Everyone wants to get to know you, you know?"

"You'll be the star of the party," I said, then saw by her expression that it was the wrong thing to say.

Kenny shot me a look before turning back to Sandy. "Don't listen to him—*I* plan on being the star of the party," he told her, and I heard her answering laugh, very soft like her voice.

Saturday night I spent about two hours getting ready for that party. I lost count of how many times I brushed my teeth and sprayed on deodorant, and I tried on and discarded four different sweatshirts before I decided I was acting like a girl on her first date and just threw on the gray one that said Go For It on the front. For all I knew she might chicken out and not show up anyway.

I found out later from Billie, who had found out from Sandy, that Sandy didn't know what was worn to a party and so she stood at her front window until she saw some of the girls arrive, and then she changed from the dress she was wearing to her jeans and a sweater like everyone else. I'll bet she wasn't brushing her teeth, though, because I'll bet she didn't have any kissing in mind. Or even getting very close to anyone.

In spite of how much time I waited I was still one of the first people at the party. I helped Billie and Kenny set up the long table in the family room with food, and then I went through Billie's record collection and put an album by The Who on her stereo. By then a lot of the kids had arrived and everyone but me was starting to fill up on the food. Billie took pity on me and got me an apple from the kitchen so that I wouldn't feel left out.

Sandy arrived all alone and she looked like someone's little sister when she walked into the room. Billie went right over to her to make her feel at home. Some of the kids had started to dance and I was really pleased when I heard Kenny ask Sandy to dance. I hadn't gotten up that much nerve myself, and anyway I'm a lousy dancer.

I could see she was telling him she couldn't dance, but then I heard Kenny say, "Anyone who can run as well as you can is bound to be able to dance," and he pulled her to the side of the room where the dancing was going on.

I could have told him that running well had nothing to do with dancing, and it was true she couldn't dance. She just kind of stood there and bounced around a little while Kenny danced circles around her, but she had a smile on her face and I thought she was enjoying herself.

I found I had no trouble at all flirting with all the girls there but Sandy. When it came to her I just didn't know what to do, so I avoided her the first part of the evening. Finally Billie came up to me and said in a low voice, "Listen, Tom, this party was for you to get to know Sandy, and you haven't even spoken to her. Now I'm going to put on a slow album and I want you to ask that girl to dance, you hear me?"

I looked over and saw that Sandy was talking to a group of runners from school and I didn't really want to butt in, but since Billie was already pushing me in that direction I didn't have much choice. I stood around listening in for a minute, then when I heard the slow music start I tapped Sandy on the arm.

"You want to dance?" I asked her, being really original.

"I'm not any good at it," she told me in her soft voice, but she looked as though she was glad to see me.

"Oh, come on," I told her, "there's nothing to dancing slow. You just kind of move from one foot to the other."

I reached for her hand and she put hers in mine, rather like a trusting child, and I led her over to where some of the others were already dancing. And since it was a slow dance, someone had put half the lights in the room out. You could still see all right, but some of the corners were dark and I could see that a few of the couples were taking advantage of that fact.

I didn't put both arms around her the way I would've done with Michelle. I put one hand on her waist and left her hand in my other one, and she reached up and put her hand on my shoulder the way it's supposed to be done. Her head came to about the middle of my chest and our bodies were a couple of inches apart.

She didn't have any trouble following me, but then I wasn't doing much. She didn't look as though she was enjoying it, though; she looked as though she was enduring it. I wondered what would happen if I kissed the top of her head the way I did with Michelle, but I didn't have the guts to find out. Anyway, I figured she'd probably never been kissed, and I didn't think the first one should be on her hair rather than her mouth.

Even thinking about kissing was a mistake because involuntarily I pulled her in closer to me, and I could feel her body stiffen. I relaxed and put a little distance between us again. "It's not so bad, is it?" I asked her.

"It's all right," she said with no enthusiasm at all.

I chuckled as though she had made a joke. "I bet you'd rather be running, though, right?"

"Wouldn't you?" She looked up at me as she said that and her eyes looked a very dark gray in the dim light.

"You know, Sandy, in order to be well-rounded, you've got to do other things besides run." And now I was coming off sounding like a mother or a school adviser.

"I don't see why," she said stubbornly.

I smiled down at her. "You really would rather be running, wouldn't you?"

She nodded, avoiding my eyes.

"Okay, come on," I told her, keeping hold of her hand and leading her out of the family room and toward the front door.

"Where're we going?"

"Running, isn't that what you want?"

She gave me such a look of delight that it was worth it to abandon a good party in favor of running in the dark. Also, running on the beach at night sounded pretty romantic to me.

We headed for the bay, which has a good stretch of beach to run on. I kept her hand in mine and she almost skipped with pleasure on our way there. The fact she was acting like a little kid at recess did occur to me, but I didn't mind. I was feeling pretty good myself. I was alone with her and that's what I had wanted.

Luckily, we were both wearing running shoes, but just about everyone wears them these days, even my mother. The beach was deserted naturally, being both December and nighttime and we decided to run a race to the end of it. Not that I had any hopes of her acting like a typical girl and letting me win. I just hoped that I was more used to running in sand than she, and this would give me some advantage.

We raced back and forth for a good twenty minutes and I could feel myself sweating freely. She was beating me easily, but she'd stop once in a while to let me catch up. Then, just when I was feeling like having a rest anyway, I tripped over something on the beach and went sprawling.

Sandy came running back to where I lay and knelt down beside me.

"Are you all right, Tom?" she asked, and I realized it was the first time she'd ever spoken my name. She said it kind of funny, more like tome than Tom, and I loved the way it sounded.

I rolled over on my back and looked up at her. "Just embarrassed, that's all."

She laughed. "Well, you better get up before I bury you in the sand."

"Go on, bury me," I challenged her.

She gave me a look of surprise, then quickly started gathering up handfuls of sand and piling them on top of me. And then, without in any way being to control the impulse, I grabbed her by the arms and pulled her down so that her face was only about an inch from mine. She didn't look worried at that point; I guess she thought I was just trying to keep her from covering me with sand.

And then, and I really shouldn't have, I pulled her even closer so that our mouths were touching and I kissed her. Her lips were soft and warm and totally unresponsive, and she never even closed her eyes, which had now widened to about the size of the full moon in the sky.

"Sorry," I muttered, letting go of her arms.

"Why did you do that?" She seemed more curious than insulted, which relieved me somewhat.

I still felt stupid, though, so I did another stupid thing. I rolled over and shoved my head in the sand as far as it would go, then began to pile sand on top of myself. I guess I was behaving like our cat who sticks his head under the bed thinking no one can see him, when in actuality his entire body is sticking out.

It turned out to be a good move, though—as Sandy started to laugh, then helped me bury myself in sand. At one point she even threw her arms around me briefly, still laughing, but it was a gesture done in fun and not at all the way I wanted her to throw her arms around me.

By that time I had sand in my hair and up my nose and seeping into my eyes and mouth, even though I had them closed, so I decided the fun was over for the night. I stood up and brushed myself off and Sandy was still looking as if she was enjoying herself. I figured the way to keep her happy was to play with her as if she were a child, even though I thought she was old enough to start acting a little more grown-up. I'm sure if I had suggested playing hide-and-seek she would have been eager, but instead I took her hand and started off the beach.

The thing is, there was something about her that brought out the protective instinct in me. Michelle was always able to take care of herself, but Sandy seemed to lean on other people. Mostly her mother and her coach, I suppose, but I was hoping maybe to be able to transfer some of that dependency to me.

"Come on, I'll take you home," I told her.

She didn't say no, or that she could get home on her own. She just let me take the lead, looking up at me every once in a while with a big smile on her face.

"I'm sorry about kissing you before," I told her when we got to her house. And I was sorry because it had been decidedly premature.

"That's okay, Tom," she murmured, looking shy at that moment.

"It's not okay—you obviously didn't want me to do it."

"I didn't mind."

"Well, it didn't seem very mutual, you know?"

She shook her head and I guess she didn't know.

I stood there looking over her head and trying to get my nerve up. Finally I figured it was now or never and if she said no, I hadn't lost anything anyway. "Do you want to go out sometime?" I asked her.

"On a date?"

I nodded.

She seemed to be thinking about it for a moment, then said, "Sure." She didn't sound enthusiastic or anything, but she hadn't said no at least.

I took a deep breath and felt my confidence return. "How about New Year's Eve?"

"I'll be in Mexico City that week—there's a meet..."

"Yeah, I forgot. How about when you get back?"

"Okay. I don't have much time, though."

"We'll find time," I assured her, then waited while she went into the house and locked the door.

I thought about going back to the party, which was still in progress, but instead I got in my car and headed for home. I was really having mixed feelings about Sandy at that point. Except for her running, which I had no trouble understanding, she was still a complete mystery to me, and the challenge was in trying to solve that mystery. Then there was the fact she was so different from any of the other girls I knew. The first time I kissed Michelle she practically melted in my arms, and after that she called me up at every opportunity. Somehow I knew Sandy wouldn't be calling me up. Not that I'm in any way criticizing Michelle. She simply acted normal, the way a girl is supposed to act. Sandy was just different, that's all. Even my little sister was more advanced socially than Sandy.

I decided I wanted to get Sandy a Christmas present but I knew I'd better keep it casual. No silver heart for her or anything that personal. One day I saw a poster in a shop in Belmont Shore for the Boston Marathon that showed some runners crossing the finish line. I almost bought it for her, then decided that men running in a marathon really had nothing to do with her. The same day I was looking in a book store in the same neighborhood and found a book on the last Olympics and decided that was just the thing. I knew some day she'd probably be in the Olypmics herself, and decided she might enjoy looking at the book. The clerk wrapped it up for me in Christmas paper and I found a Christmas card with one of those funny cats and a sarcastic message inside, and I signed my name and planned on taking it over to her on Christmas Eve.

When Christmas Eve came, though, and I drove by her house to deliver my present, the house was all closed up. I stopped by Billie's to say hello, she told me Sandy and her mother had already left for Mexico.

Christmas was pretty good. My folks gave me a small color TV set for my room that I could also take away with me to college. I also got a bunch of clothes, as usual, and some new track shoes. Chrissie bought me a couple of record albums and I was listening to them that afternoon when Kenny came by. We had never exchanged Christmas presents before, but this year he had a package for me, and without even thinking about it I went to my room and took the card off Sandy's book and handed the package to Kenny. He liked the book, I could tell, and I liked the stopwatch he gave me. He hung around a while listening to my new albums, and then he had to go home to dinner and I had to go with my family over to my grandparents' house for dinner.

I didn't know what to do about New Year's Eve. My parents were going out, even Chrissie was going to a party, and I really didn't feel like spending the night sitting around the house by myself. There's not even anything good on TV on New Year's Eve.

Michelle's friend Jannine, the one who always flirts, called me up during the week to invite me to a New Year's Eve party she was having.

I guess I didn't sound very interested, because she said, "I told Michelle I was inviting you and she didn't mind, Tom."

"It might be a little uncomfortable," I said.

"Come on, Tom, everyone breaks up at one time or another. If she doesn't mind, I don't see why you should."

"Do I have to bring a date?"

"Lots of kids are coming without dates, don't worry about it."

So I decided to take her advice and not worry about it. I didn't see why Michelle and I couldn't be friends and it was stupid to keep trying to avoid her. And any party would be a lot better than spending the night alone at home.

I did worry a little about Jannine. As far as I knew, she wasn't going with anyone, and when I'd gone with Michelle she'd always been after me. I was afraid that things might get a little sticky, but then the worst that would happen would be I'd dance with Jannine, and after all, I had to dance with someone, I supposed. If I couldn't dance with Sandy, it didn't much matter to me who I danced with.

Kenny was going to a different party but when I got to Jannine's, I found a lot of my friends were there. She has a great house for a party. Her parents had converted a three-car garage into a family room, which made it completely separate from the rest of the house, so we could make as much noise as we wanted and not disturb her family, who was staying home that night.

There was a nice spread of food and a lot of room for dancing, and she had a setup that flashed lights around the room just like they have at discos, so I've heard. I've never been to a discotheque.

Except for greeting me, when I arrived, it turned out that Jannine practically ignored me. This made me wonder whether she had even been interested in me or whether she'd just wanted what Michelle had. I was feeding my face when Michelle and Mike came in. I had decided to go off my health diet over the holidays and was really getting into the food when I saw them come in and I caught Michelle's eye.

She nodded to me, really cool, as though we'd never even gone out together, and when they came over to get some food, Mike said, "How's it going, Tom?" which was a lot more than Michelle said.

Then I saw Michelle looking around as if to see whether Sandy was there, so I headed over to where some of the track team were talking in a group. One of the runners, Ann Harris, was there, and I struck up a conversation with her hoping that Michelle would think we were together. Although why I cared what Michelle thought, I don't know.

Ann was looking really good in a green corduroy jump-suit that set off her red hair and green eyes, and even when I went with Michelle I used to think I wouldn't mind going out with her. She was also a good runner, and this year, for some reason, she was doing about twice as well as she'd done before. I had meant to ask her what her secret was, but then I got so involved with Sandy, I forgot all about it.

I asked her to dance when a slow song came on and about thirty seconds into the dance I decided to find out. Anyhow, there wasn't anything else to talk about with her as I didn't know her all that well.

"Tell me something, Ann?" I asked, holding her a little away from me so that we could talk.

"What do you want to know, Tom?"

"How did your running improve so drastically? You on a health-food kick, too?"

She shook her head, her green eyes smiling up at me. "I took up dancing."

"Dancing?" I looked around the floor as though she meant that kind of dancing.

"Ballet," she said.

"And that helped your running?"

"It sure seemed to. I think the best thing is the way it develops the muscles, but it's also improved my style. I have films my dad took of me running before and after the dancing, and there's sure an improvement in the way I move."

I tried to look interested even though I knew nothing about ballet and didn't really want to know anything. "That's fine for you girls," I finally said, "but I guess us guys are out of luck."

She chuckled. "The coach made three guys on the football team join the class. He told them they were too clumsy by half, and I guess they improved because he finally let them quit."

"Which guys?" I asked her, wondering why I hadn't heard about that. When she named them I laughed out loud. I sure couldn't picture those mooses doing ballet.

"You ought to try it, Tom—it couldn't hurt."

"You're not catching me out there in some tutu," I protested.

"You can wear your running shorts."

"Naw, I'd feel really stupid."

"You wouldn't feel so stupid if it improved your running, would you?"

"I'll think about it," I told her, not wanting to get into an argument about ballet.

"Sandy's in the class."

I kind of stopped dancing for a moment, wondering whether she knew about me and Sandy. But then what was there to know?

"You know, Sandy Smith?" she asked me. "The one who works out with us?"

"Yeah, I know who she is," I answered really casually.

"Sandy swears by it," she went on, "and if it's done that much for her, I figure it can't hurt."

I was beginning to reassess my thinking about ballet. It would be one more place where I could see Sandy. "When do you take the class?" I asked her.

"Saturday mornings. Why don't you come, Tom? You chicken?"

If there's one thing I can't stand, it's being called chicken. "I just might," I told her, then pulled her in closer to me to cut off any further conversation.

I looked around the room as we danced and saw that Michelle and Mike were dancing, wrapped around each other so closely that they looked like one person. I felt a twinge of annoyance at that, then told myself I had no right to feel annoyed about anything Michelle did. But we'd gone together a long time and I still felt somewhat possessive of her.

Later, when Ann and I were getting a Coke, I saw Mike take a pint bottle out of his back pocket and offer some to Michelle before drinking down some himself. This really bothered me, but there was nothing I could do about it. Liquor wasn't being served at the party and anyway, none of us who go out for sports ever drink except maybe once in a while—sometimes I'd take a swallow of my dad's beer. But I had heard that Mike was a drinker and I was afraid maybe Michelle was into that now. I kept an eye on her after that and noticed she was getting progressively sillier.

At one point, she started dancing all by herself, throwing her body around as though she didn't care who was looking. I just couldn't take it any more and I went over to her and grabbed her by the arm.

"Why don't you cool it, Michelle?"

She whirled on me, a look of total fury on her face. "Get your hands off me, Cunningham," she hissed, her face contorted by her rage.

I dropped my hand and just looked at her.

"Where do you get off telling me what to do, anyway? Where's your little girlfriend? Isn't she allowed out on dates yet?"

I was just standing there feeling really sad that Michelle seemed to hate me, when Mike came over and asked Michelle what the problem was.

"No problem, darling," she drawled, moving really close to him so that he was almost forced to put his arms around her. And that "darling" sounded really phony coming from her. She had never called me darling; if she had, I would've laughed.

"I think she's had too much to drink," I said to Mike, then went over to where Ann was talking to some of her friends. Just when I got to her, someone started shouting that it was midnight, and right away everyone started kissing, and since no one was kissing Ann and it seemed the thing to do, I leaned down and gave her what I figured was a nice, brotherly kiss on the lips. The way she kissed me back wasn't quite so sisterly, but it was a nice kiss and I began to be glad I'd gone to the party after all instead of staying home and feeling sorry for myself.

When the kissing and cheering were all over, I saw that Michelle and Mike were still kissing, and as I watched it turned into what must have been the longest kiss in history. The way Michelle was behaving was kind of making me sick, so I asked Ann if she wanted to leave the party and get a hamburger or something. I guess she thought I was nuts since there was still plenty of food at the party, but she said okay, so we headed out of there before anyone could ask where we were going.

She was a nice girl and I enjoyed her company, but Michelle had been a nice girl, too, and I'd always had a lot of fun with her. But you can't help who you fall in love with, and I guess for me it was Sandy, so even though I could tell that Ann was expecting me to ask her out when I took her home, I didn't. I did half promise to show up at her next ballet class, though.

That night in bed I thought more about Michelle than I did about Sandy. I was worried she was going to get a bad reputation going around with Mike, and I was hoping I wasn't responsible. I guess I was, though. I guess we have to take responsibility for all our actions.

Chapter Five

January will probably turn out to be the month I made the biggest fool of myself in my whole life.

The first day back at school I ran into Ann in the halls and she reminded me that I'd said I'd come to her ballet class the following Saturday. What had seemed like not a bad idea at the party, now seemed like a very stupid idea indeed.

At lunch, I sat with Kenny, and as soon as we were finished eating, I said to him, "Hey, Kenny, you doing anything Saturday?"

"You got another track meet lined up for us?"

"No, Sandy's only one this month is in New York, and that's a few weeks off."

"I'm not going to New York."

"I'm not, either, but I heard something good—something that would help us at track."

"Tell me about it" was all he said, and he didn't sound too enthusiastic.

"It's this dance class."

He looked a little interested and then I remembered he liked to dance. Only it wasn't ballet he liked to do.

"I could get into jazz dancing," he said.

"It's not exactly jazz, Kenny."

"What exactly is it?"

I didn't know quite how to put it. Ballet just didn't sound like something two jocks would do. "Ann tells me it improved her speed and style."

"Yeah, she's a whole lot faster this year, I've noticed."

"I just thought it might be something you'd be interested in."

"You didn't mention what kind of dancing it was."

"Well, it's more classical."

Kenny gave me a suspicious look. "I hope you're not talking about ballet."

I managed to choke on my milk.

"You *are* talking about ballet, aren't you? You actually expect me to go to a *ballet* class?"

"Some of the football players went."

"Don't put me in the same class as football players. Football players were never noted for their brains."

"Wouldn't you like to be more graceful when you jump?" I asked him, grabbing at straws.

"What're you talking about, man? Why, I've been told I'm as graceful as a cat!"

"I'm serious, Kenny."

"So am I, Thomas. There's no way you're going to get me to go to a ballet class, so quit wasting your time." He paused a moment, then broke into a smile. "Is it Annie Harris? You interested in her?"

"No. Sandy's in the class, too," I admitted. "But I'd really like to see if it helps." Now I was defending something I sure didn't want to try.

"Listen, friend—I'll go to meets with you to see her, I'll even have my girlfriend have parties so you can get to know her, but I put my foot down when it comes to ballet. No way, man—no way!"

I thought maybe he was just putting up an initial protest so I wouldn't think he was actually eager to join a ballet class, but by the end of the week when he was still saying no, I realized that I was going to have to show up at that ballet class all alone.

The reaction I got at the dinner table when I broke the news to my family wasn't all that great, either. My father just sat there looking at me as though he'd been wrong about me and my mother was trying very hard not to laugh. Chrissie offered to loan me her leotard and tights, which broke everyone up, and then, thank heavens, the discussion was dropped and Chrissie once more became the center of attention.

On Saturday morning when I went down to the kitchen in my running shorts and top, my mom suggested I wear sweats to the class instead, so I went back upstairs and changed. The only thing I wondered about was what kind of shoes to wear, finally settling on running shoes. If I could run in them, I figured I could also dance in them.

The ballet studio was located in a shopping center in Los Altos, and the hardest thing I ever did was walk through the door of that studio. I was early, unusual for me, but I figured it was better than walking in late and having all eyes turned to watch my entrance. A class of little girls who were maybe ten years' old, was just ending, and these kids in their little pink and white outfits made me feel like the worst kind of imposter.

As I was standing by the desk in front waiting to talk to the teacher, Sandy and her mother came in. Sandy's eyes widened when she saw me and her mother said, "You do get around, don't you?" I didn't want to get smart with her mother, so I didn't answer that, but I asked Sandy how she'd done in Mexico City. The altitude had bothered her and she hadn't broken any records, but she'd placed first in both events she'd entered.

Then Ann came and broke into a big smile when she saw me. "So you did show up, huh? I figured you'd chicken out, Tom."

"Listen, if it'll improve my running," I muttered, noticing that Sandy was looking from me to Ann. It was too much to hope that she was jealous, but at least she knew I wasn't there just because of her.

The teacher, who was called Lisa, wasn't any older than her late twenties and she had this long ponytail that hung clear down to her waist. She was also dressed in pink and white but on her it looked spectacular. I had to drag my eyes away from her figure while she told me I could take the first class at no charge to see whether I liked it or not, then asked me to remove my shoes before going onto the wood floor.

So there I was in my bare feet and sweats amongst this group of girls who all seemed to know what they were doing. I felt big and clumsy and really stupid.

The first thing we did in class was to stand in a line along a long, mirrored wall, holding onto this railing attached to it, and do a few things with our feet. They were called positions and I never quite got the hang of them. Plus all the attention was focused on our feet and mine looked very large and dumb and I wished I'd been allowed to leave my shoes on. For all I knew my feet probably smelled.

But that wasn't half as bad as what came next. I tried to copy the girl in front of me as we did weird things like lift our legs up onto the railing, something that made me feel as though I were about to split in two. Maybe girls can do that stuff, but it was really painful for me. I had a feeling I wouldn't be able to walk properly for a week. Some of the girls were able to get their legs way up over their heads and it really made me mad that I couldn't do the same. So I tried. And the result was I fell right down and landed on my rear end and I really couldn't blame everyone for laughing. I tried to laugh too, but it's not so easy to laugh when you think you've been bruised for life.

After what seemed like ten hours doing that, but which was probably only ten minutes, we were told to line up in the middle of the floor, and then after that all the instructions were given in French. I know about three words in French and not one of them was used. The teacher would shout out some French word, and all the girls would do some dance step, very quickly, then get back into line. By the time I caught onto what they were doing, I'd be doing the step all alone—and very badly—while everyone else watched me. I think the girls were enjoying my being in the class—I was like a comedy relief.

It was a fiasco. A total fiasco. I did as well as I could, I honestly did, but nothing worked out right and all I was doing was publicly making a fool of myself just to be in the same class with Sandy. I honestly didn't feel that any of the stuff was going to help my running in any way. All it was making me do was want to run very fast as far from that class as I could get.

When it was all over, I thanked Lisa and told her I didn't think the class was for me. I only hoped that the word wouldn't get around to the guys at school that I had even gone there once. I didn't even talk to Ann, who had gotten me into it in the first place, but I walked Sandy out to the parking lot.

"You want to go out tonight?" I asked her. She hesitated and I added, "That is, if I can still move tonight. That's the hardest exercise I've ever done."

"Does that mean you're not going to be a ballet dancer?" she asked me, which I think was the first humorous remark I'd ever heard her make.

"I seriously doubt it," I told her. "How about tonight? You want to go see a movie?"

"I guess so," she said, which didn't do a whole lot for my ego.

"Great. I'll pick you up about seven-thirty?"

She nodded and her mother pulled up then, so I left before she could change her mind.

Due to her shyness and lack of conversational skills, I decided to see if Kenny and Billie wanted to double-date with us. I figured she'd feel less shy with Billie around than being all alone with me.

I drove by Kenny's house and he was out in the front yard mowing the lawn.

"How was ballet?" he yelled at me, and I quickly looked around to see if any of his neighbors had heard him.

"I think you would have done better," I told him. "I'm just not a dancer."

"Made a fool of yourself, huh?"

I started to deny this, then finally nodded. "Yeah. That plus every muscle in my body is killing me."

"What you need is a good massage."

"You going to give me one?"

"Me? I don't know anything about massage."

He agreed to double that night and we decided we'd see the new Woody Allen movie, even though I think he's gotten weird lately instead of funny. I said I'd drive since I thought it was a little soon to be in the back seat of a car alone with Sandy. I thought this was probably her first date and I wanted her to enjoy herself so that she'd be willing to go out with me again. At least, I had one advantage—I don't think any other guys were even asking her out. The

combination of her looking so young and being so famous
would probably put most guys off.

Sandy looked really different that night when I picked her
up. She was dressed in soft gray-blue leather pants and a
jacket she'd been give for Christmas, and she wore a navy-
blue turtleneck sweater underneath. It was her hair and face,
though, that really surprised me. She had done something
with her hair—maybe curled it, I don't know—and it was all
full and fluffy around her face. And she wore makeup for
the first time that I'd ever seen. She had something around
her eyes that made them stand out and also some lipstick. I
thought at first she'd used blusher on her cheeks, but it was
cold out that night, so it might just have been that.

She looked older somehow, or maybe it was just the way
she'd really look when she got older. I could see Kenny and
Billie giving her looks when we picked them up at Billie's
house, but neither of them said anything, and all I said was
that she looked nice, and I would have said that anyway just
to make her feel good about herself.

A lot of the kids from school were at the movie and I
could see some of them checking out the fact I was with
Sandy. It was the first time we'd been out together in public
and I guess everyone had been wondering what I'd been
doing with myself since breaking up with Michelle. I was
glad for my own ego that Sandy looked good, but I hoped
she didn't look so good all the other guys would start coming on to her.

Kenny and Billie got popcorn and Cokes but I was back
on my health diet, so Sandy and I had to listen to them
crunch their way through the movie. Kenny and Billie had
been going together long enough that they didn't get all cozy
in the movies, and I spent the first hour wondering whether
I should put my arm around Sandy. I was spending so much
time wondering about it, I couldn't even tell you what the

movie was about. I finally edged my arm around the back of her seat and she didn't flinch or anything, so about three quarters of the way into the movie I finally let it drop on her shoulders. She moved a little to get more comfortable but didn't seem to mind.

Now I know all this makes me sound like a real novice when it comes to girls, but that's just not the case. Normally, I'd have my arm around the girl two minutes into the movie and I'd figure if she was out with me to begin with, she'd know that was part of the deal. The same goes for a good-night kiss or two. But I guess with Sandy, I was still afraid of scaring her off, plus I had real feelings for her and I wanted things to be the way she wanted them. Only I just couldn't get a clear picture of what she actually wanted.

I guess the movie was fairly funny because everyone was laughing but me, and that's only because I was concentrating on Sandy and not the movie. It felt so good to be just sitting there with her, my arm around her and her soft hair occasionally brushing against my face. Even when my arm got tired from being in the position, I didn't remove it.

After the movie we stopped by Hamburger Henry's as Kenny and Billie were still hungry. We were sitting all cozy in a booth when Michelle and Mike came in and sat down in the only empty booth in the place, which was right across from ours. I said hi to them, and Mike said hi back, but Michelle just ignored me, although I could see she was checking out Sandy. I was suddenly glad that Sandy looked so good and was dressed great. Michelle didn't look all that good, I noticed. She seemed to be losing weight, her eyes had circles under them, and she wasn't dressed as well as she used to dress. I figured that was all due to Mike's influence on her and wondered why she'd picked him to go out with, when she could've dated almost any guy in the school.

I dropped Kenny off at Billie's house while I took Sandy home. When I walked her to the door she asked, "Why was that girl staring at me in the restaurant?"

"That was Michelle," I told her.

"Why was she staring at me?"

"I used to go with her."

"She was your girlfriend?"

I nodded.

"She's very pretty. Did she prefer that other boy to you?"

"No. It was more my fault that we broke up." More your fault, actually, I thought of saying to her, but I didn't think she'd understand.

"You don't like her anymore?"

"Not like that, no. As a matter of fact, I prefer you now."

That little piece of information didn't seem to interest her much, or maybe she just already knew. "Thank you, Tom, I had a very nice time," she said, getting out her house key and putting it into the lock.

"What're you doing tomorrow?" I asked her.

"I have to study."

"On a Sunday?"

She gave me a serious look. "I don't get much time during the week so I have to catch up on weekends. I'm missing a lot of school with these out-of-town meets...." Her voice trailed off and I nodded my understanding.

"Come here," I said, "let's see if you can give me a real kiss."

I held out my arms but she didn't rush into them as I had hoped. She looked a little tentative and a little scared, but she moved in my direction and actually tilted her face up for a kiss.

"Put your arms around me, Sandy."

She looked to the left toward Billie's house. "Don't you have to get Kenny?"

"Kenny can wait. Believe it or not, Kenny and Billie are probably over there kissing themselves."

She chuckled at that and actually put her arms up and around my neck. She still wasn't going to make the first move as far as kissing goes, though, so I lowered my head, put my arms around her, and closed my mouth over hers. Hers was totally unmoving.

I pulled away. "Come on, Sandy. Can't you act like you enjoy it?"

"I was enjoying it."

"Kiss me back, okay? Just move your lips around, or something."

I kissed her again and this time she kissed me in return. I could have stood there all night like that, just holding her in my arms and kissing her. But being a good guy, I finally moved my mouth from hers and just stood there hugging her for a moment before releasing her. "Now that wasn't so bad, was it?"

She smiled. "It was okay."

"But you'd rather be running, right?"

She gave me an impish grin. "Right."

I turned the key in the lock and shoved the door open. "Get in the house before I challenge you to a race. I'll call you tomorrow, okay?"

"Okay," she said, then closed the door. No lingering farewells, no loving looks—no nothing, really, although I had high hopes. After all, I was getting somewhere, I told myself. I'd gotten to know her, I'd taken her out on a date, I'd even kissed her and she'd returned the kiss, albeit reluctantly. Give me another month and I was sure we'd be going together.

Of course next year, I'd be away at college, but UCLA wasn't that far. She could come up for weekends. Heck, it wouldn't be bad to be dating a celebrity and have her visit me on campus, although her celebrity wasn't what I liked about her. Well, it was sort of what I liked about her, her running skill, I mean, but it didn't matter to me whether she was famous or not. And the fact that she was different. She didn't flirt, she didn't even act interested. But I was sure I'd change that. Soon we'd be a couple, just like Michelle and I had been.

"Billie says you're wasting your time," Kenny said to me as soon as he got in the car.

"What're you talking about?"

"Sandy, that's what."

"What'd Billie say exactly?"

"She said that Sandy wasn't ready for guys, that you were rushing her."

I gave an exaggerated sigh. "Rushing her's the last thing I'm doing."

"Billie says she's got a one-track mind and that one track is strictly track. If you get what I mean with all those tracks in there."

"That's not true, she's interested in other things."

"Like what?"

"Well, she's in that ballet class?"

"Not because she wants to be a dancer, man; she's in there to improve her running." Then Kenny added, "You're just perverse, that's all."

"What's that supposed to mean?"

"It means you have to hit on the one girl in school who won't fall all over herself just to get a date with you. You're interested in her simply because she's not interested in you."

"I think I can get her interested in me; in fact I think I've already started. She went out with me, didn't she?"

"Billie says that's probably 'cause she didn't know how to say no."

"Oh, come on!"

"Listen, Billie said that, not me. Don't go yelling at me."

"I've never felt this way about a girl before," I admitted to him.

"You mean frustrated?"

"No, I mean I really have strong feelings about her."

"I remember when you used to say the same thing about Michelle."

"I was younger then."

"Yeah, a few months younger. Who you kidding, Tom?"

"I swear, Kenny, I didn't feel the same about Michelle. I don't even know what I saw in her anymore. Did you see how she looked tonight?"

"I have a feeling that's your fault."

"Oh, come on!"

"Look, just because you stopped liking her doesn't mean it was mutual, you know. She doesn't look all that happy to me."

"Then she should quit seeing Stern."

"Maybe she figured you'd rescue her from him."

"Michelle's a big girl; she can rescue herself."

Kenny seemed annoyed with me at that point and didn't say anything more until I dropped him off at his house. Then I started kidding around with him and everything was all right again. I didn't want to quarrel with Kenny. He's a friend and friends last forever; girlfriends somehow never last that long.

I called Sandy the next day but found talking to her on the phone wasn't very satisfactory. She'd answer questions put to her but wouldn't offer any of her own, and her answers were usually only a yes or a no. I realized after I hung up that she never asked me anything about myself. I didn't know whether it was from lack of interest or just her shyness, but I was determined to start telling her about myself

anyway. Not that there was all that much to tell, but I'd
done a few things in my seventeen years.

The next Saturday night Sandy agreed to go out with me
again, but it turned out to be raining really hard that night
so we just stayed home at her place and watched a show on
her new TV. Her mother was out and we had the place to
ourselves but nothing much happened.

She lived in this really small house that made me think at
first they were poor. But then I mentioned to my dad where
she lived and he told me real estate in Naples was worth
about ten times as much as where we lived, so then I started
thinking of her as affluent. Of course, her mother worked
in real estate and maybe she had gotten a good deal.

Sandy showed me her room and that was a big surprise.
It didn't look like any kid's room that I'd ever seen. All it
had was a small bed, neatly made, a chest of drawers, a desk
and a chair. Except for some of her schoolbooks on her
desk, there wasn't any stuff sitting around the room at all.
Nothing. There wasn't even a picture or a poster on the wall.
You can tell a whole lot about most girls by their rooms, but
not Sandy. There wasn't even a stuffed animal on her bed!

Then she showed me her workout room and I guessed that
was where she spent her time when she wasn't sleeping or
studying. It had an exercycle, a rowing machine, a chin-
ning bar and a bench with weights. She even had a stereo, so
she could exercise to music. We fooled around for a while
with the equipment until I found out she could do all the
stuff better than I could, even the weights. Then we went
into the living room and watched some TV. That's about it,
except I got to kiss her good-night again, and this time she
kissed me back without my asking.

The next weekend she was at Madison Square Gardens in
New York for the Millrose Games, the biggest indoor track
event of the year. For a couple of weeks before it, her pic-

ture was in the LA papers all the time and I cut out each picture and article about her for my bulletin board, which was getting pretty crowded. I figured if she ever saw my room she'd be really surprised.

There was a tape on television of the games and my dad watched it with me. It was really strange watching a girl I was going out with on television, it didn't seem real. What was real was her breaking records in both events and being the star of the games.

My dad kept saying, "That's the girl you're going out with?" and I kept nodding my head, trying not to let my pride show.

Sunday night, I kept trying to call her on the phone but the line was always busy. Later, I found out lots of reporters were trying to get her for interviews.

A few days later a national news magazine came out with her picture on the cover, and kids at school who hadn't known who she was before, sure knew then. Some of them came up to me in the hall and asked if I was the one going out with Sandy Smith. It got so she was better known around the school than I was. I didn't mind, though. She was well-known for a good reason, with me it was just that I'd been around the school for almost four years.

My mom surprised me by having the magazine cover of Sandy framed for me, and when I came home from school one day it was hanging in my room. The article in the magazine had said it was predicted she would become the greatest woman runner of all time, barring injuries, and my mom asked me when she was going to meet this phenomenon. I told her I'd have Sandy over to dinner as soon as I could arrange it.

Something I haven't mentioned—during all this time my grades were steadily improving. I guess it was because I wasn't spending all my evenings on the telephone anymore, nor was I dating nearly as much. When I was going with Michelle, we'd been practically inseparable.

I kept thinking that maybe by summer, Sandy and I'd be inseparable.

Chapter Six

In February, Wilson High had a Valentine's Day dance and I figured I'd ask Sandy if she wanted to go. I don't really like dances much and Michelle used to have to drag me to them with dire threats if I were to refuse, but now that there was no pressure on me to attend, I found I wanted to go to one with Sandy. Maybe I just wanted the other kids at school to know we were a couple, which is how I pictured us.

I had reckoned without Sandy. "No, I don't think so," she said to me when I asked her.

"Why not, Sandy? You'll have fun."

"You know I'm not a good dancer."

"Neither am I."

Her voice lowered until it had a trace of huskiness in it. "Kids will talk to me; kids I don't know."

"What's the matter with that? That's called being friendly."

She kind of shrugged and looked unhappy, and I asked her what was the matter.

"Everyone talks to me at school now, kids I don't even know. They're not interested in me, Tom, just in the fact I had my picture on the cover of a magazine."

"You've got fans, Sandy—you're famous," I joked with her, but she didn't look amused.

"Well, I don't like it," she murmured, her eyes downcast. "I hate it when people crowd around me and ask me questions."

I still wasn't taking her seriously. "Hey, you'll have to get used to it. Don't the reporters hassle you at the meets?"

"They're just doing their job, they don't bother me. But with the kids it's just curiosity, and I don't like being just an object of curiosity."

"Okay, look, we don't have to go to the dance. As a matter of fact, I don't even like dances. How about coming over to my place for dinner, my folks would like to meet you? After, we can catch a movie if you want."

She agreed to that but not with any enthusiasm.

My family's reactions to Sandy's coming to dinner were mixed. Mom just wanted to know if Sandy and I ate the same kind of food, in which case she'd serve something vegetarian. I told her just to make her spaghetti, which was terrific. Dad seemed impressed. He'd talked about her a lot since seeing her on TV and I cautioned him not to bombard her with questions, telling him how shy she was. Chrissie was excited about seeing Sandy in person. She had watched the mounting collection of newspaper pictures of Sandy going up on my wall and she couldn't understand my interest in a girl who wasn't even as pretty as *she* was, which were her exact words. Chrissie hasn't as yet learned the virtue of modesty.

We ate informally in the dining room, and along with the spaghetti Mom had made salad and garlic bread, which is my all-time favorite dinner. With a rather boyish gesture, Sandy shook my parents' hands when introduced, much to everyone's surprise. I wondered if that was something she'd picked up at the track meets.

Sandy said all of about two words while we ate. Chrissie was unusually silent, watching Sandy with sidelong glances from her seat beside her at the table, which left Mom and Dad to carry on the bulk of the conversation with a little help from me.

After dinner, my big-mouthed sister said, "Why don't you show Sandy your room, Tom?"

"Shut up, Chrissie!"

"You'd just love his room, Sandy, make him show it to you." Her look of innocence made me want to strangle her.

Sandy looked up at me. "Could I see it, Tom?"

"It's a mess," I told her, "and I think we ought to get started if we want to catch the eight o'clock show."

"It'll only take a minute; I'd really like to see it."

I could see my parents exchanging amused glances as I took Sandy upstairs. Of course the first thing that hit her eyes when we looked in my room was one wall now almost entirely filled with pictures of her. In the place of honor, over my bed, was the framed magazine cover of her.

Sandy walked into the room for a closer look, her eyes traveling over the wall. "You even have some from before I knew you," she remarked.

"Yeah, well, I'd seen you working out with us."

With her back to me, she said, "Is that why you want to go out with me? Because I get my picture in the papers?"

"No, Sandy. I was interested before you got your picture in the paper, that's why I cut it out. Ask Kenny, he'll tell you."

"But *why* were you interested? You didn't even know me."

"I just knew I wanted to know you."

"But what was it that interested you? My running?" She turned around to face me and I could see she was dead serious.

"I guess it was at first. The first time I saw you, you went by me on the track like I was standing still. And then...I don't know, there was something about you that was different."

"Different how?"

"Ah, Sandy, I don't know. Just different. Different from the other girls I've known."

"But *how*?"

"Give me a break, Sandy—I don't know. Why are you interested in me?"

"What makes you think I am?"

That really stopped me, and then I saw the gleam in her gray eyes, and I saw that for the very first time she was flirting with me. Maybe she wasn't so different after all, I was thinking to myself. "Why do you go out with me?" I asked her.

She shrugged. "Because you ask me."

"Oh, so you'd go out with any guy who asked you?"

She smiled. "Maybe."

I felt at that moment that it was the closest we'd ever been. Just standing there kidding around, something we'd never really done before. I walked over to her and gave her a big hug, lifting her right up off her feet. "If I catch you going out with any other guy..."

"What would you do?"

"If I were you I wouldn't try to find out."

She laughed aloud. "Don't worry, Tom—no one's asked me out anyway."

"Good. Make sure it stays that way." I gave her a kiss on her nose, then set her back down on her feet. "Good, now let's go to the movies. Unless you've changed your mind and want to go to the dance."

"Did you really want to go?"

I shook my head. "No, I just thought maybe you'd want to."

"I'm okay with just you and me, but I'm not very good with groups of people," she admitted to me.

"That's called the freshman syndrome," I told her. "You'll get over it."

"I bet your little sister's not like that."

"Chrissie's a born show-off—she thrives on groups of people."

In the car, she said, "I like your family. They seem really happy."

"One big happy family," I quipped.

"I'm serious. I think it'd be nice to have a family like that."

"You're welcome to adopt Chrissie," I offered. I'd never asked her about her family, but since she was being so forthcoming I thought I'd give it a try. "Do you ever see your dad?" I asked.

She shook her head. "I don't even remember him. He lives in Iowa now and is remarried and has three kids."

"Do you keep in touch with him?"

She shook her head again, clearly not wanting to talk about it. "My mom and I are very close," she finally said.

"Yeah, I imagine—just the two of you together and all."

She was quiet for the rest of the drive and I was sure I'd shattered her earlier good mood, but we both held hands and laughed a lot in the movie and afterward she seemed back to normal. We stopped by Hamburger Henry's, which was probably a mistake as a lot of the kids from the dance were there, including Michelle and Mike, neither of whom would speak to me.

When I got home that night everyone else was in bed and I watched a little of the late show before going to bed myself. I hadn't been in bed more than ten minutes when the phone rang and I picked it up before it would wake anyone else.

It was Michelle and she sounded like she was crying. "Will you talk to me for a few minutes, Tom?" she asked.

"I don't know, Michelle—I mean, when you won't even speak to me in public...."

"I still love you, Tom."

"Oh, Michelle..."

"I do. I can't help it."

"Listen, you'll get over it."

"When? It's been months and it's not getting any easier."

What do you say when someone says something like that? I was just lying there wishing she'd never called. "You seem happy enough with Mike," I pointed out to her.

"Mike's okay—he's not as bad as you think."

"Good—I'm happy for you."

"But I'm not in love with him. What did I do wrong, Tom? I try to figure it out, but I just can't. One day we were happy together and the next you had just lost all interest. Was it something I did?"

"It wasn't you, Michelle—you were fine."

"If I was fine, why did it happen?"

"I guess I just didn't really love you."

There was a long silence. Then, "If you didn't love me, why did you tell me you did all the time?"

"I thought I did at the time."

"And now you think you've found true love?" She sounded bitter at that point and I couldn't blame her. I was saying all the wrong things and I knew it, but I couldn't seem to find the right things to say.

"I wish we could be friends, Michelle."

"I tell you I love you and you say let's be friends. I thought I knew you, Tom, but maybe I was wrong."

"I'm sure you and Mike..." I began to say, but she interrupted with a nasty "Forget it!" and hung up on me. I hate to be hung up on and was tempted to call her back and hang up on her, but then I decided I was above such childish behavior and just hung up the phone on my end.

I couldn't get to sleep for a long time after that. I tried to turn my thoughts to Sandy, but it didn't work and instead I kept thinking about Michelle and me.

The first time I'd seen her at school I thought she was the prettiest girl I'd ever seen. I never figured I had a chance with her, though, because she was dating some pretty high-powered guys and was being given the rush by a bunch of others. Although only a freshman, she had just walked in and practically taken over the school. Everywhere I went in the school I would see her, always surrounded by a group of students. Then I lucked out the second semester and had her in my Spanish class.

I usually sat in the back of the class for something like Spanish in the hopes I would be overlooked and never get called on, but when I saw she sat somewhere in the center I managed to get a seat next to hers for the second class. I tried my cool act at first, totally ignoring her, but it didn't work because she didn't seem to even notice my presence.

By about the fifth class with her I was getting desperate and managed a fake trip in the aisle that just happened to send her books flying off her desk. I very helpfully picked them up for her and she thanked me with a smile. A smile so beautiful I fantasized about it for days.

After that she said hello to me in class, but it didn't seem to go any further. The next thing I tried was cutting class one day so that I could call her at home that night and ask her for the homework assignment. She was very businesslike on the phone and I didn't think I was getting anywhere, so I happened to drop into the conversation that I was on the track team and was she going to the big meet the following Friday night.

She said she hadn't thought about it but if she wasn't doing anything else, maybe she would.

That Friday night I scanned the stands for a glimpse of her, and when I finally found her I went right out and won the race. The adrenaline was flowing more from her presence than from any excitement over the race.

Afterward, I looked for her but she'd already gone. In the next Spanish class I had with her she told me how impressed she'd been and how she liked watching track more than she thought she would.

"I could follow it a lot better than football," she admitted to me in a low voice, then, when the teacher frowned at her, she wrote me a note saying the same thing.

I wrote her back saying football was great when you understood the game.

She wrote me back saying maybe, but she didn't understand it so she was bored to death.

I wrote her back saying I could explain it to her in twenty minutes if she was interested. When I passed her that note I figured it would be the end of it, and I pretended a great interest in what the teacher was saying. But since what she was saying was in Spanish, I wouldn't have understood it even if I had actually been paying attention.

I was really floored when the note came back to me saying only "When?"

"At your convenience," I wrote back.

"How about after school today?" she wrote.

So, for the very first time, I missed track workout that day and met her after school instead. I wasn't old enough to drive then, which I figured put me at a disadvantage with her as most girls like to date boys with cars, but it wasn't a long walk to a nearby McDonald's. We went there and sat at one of the tables and consumed about four Cokes each while I explained to her the intricacies of football.

Well, Michelle was about as good at learning football as I was at learning Spanish, so while she pretended to understand me, she later confessed that she wasn't even paying attention to what I was saying. She said that mostly she was just having fun gazing into my beautiful blue eyes. That's what she said—that's not my personal opinion of my eyes, you understand, which are just your ordinary blue.

Well, that day went pretty well. I was really glad when I found out how close to me she lived, but I still didn't have the guts to ask her out for a date. Where was I going to take her, for a walk? None of my friends had their driver's licenses yet and it seemed kind of juvenile to have my dad take us somewhere and pick us up. I counted without Michelle, however.

The next time we had Spanish together she wrote me a note saying she thought maybe she'd understand football better if I taught her how to play. I wrote her back asking her what she was doing on Saturday, and when she wrote back "Nothing," I finished off the note by saying I'd be over at her house at ten in the morning, complete with football, and that she should wear old clothes.

She read it quickly, then gave me a big smile and nodded her head. I guess I knew at that moment I had a chance with her, and I was so happy I could only grin back. After all, she couldn't really be interested in playing football, could she?

I was pretty sure she wasn't; not many girls like to spend their Saturdays throwing a ball around.

I was there fifteen minutes early with my football and she was ready and waiting. Luckily, she had a big backyard with lots of grass and no swimming pool, so we went back there and for about three hours I tried to teach her how to throw and catch a football and how to kick it. Then I suggested that we concentrate for a while on tackling, but she just gave me a knowing look and said that she'd rather fix me some lunch if I was interested.

After lunch, I thought maybe she wanted me to leave, so I got up and said something inane, but she just smiled and asked if I wanted to play some Ping-Pong. By then I'd met her mom and dad, who were both really nice, and her two little brothers who couldn't figure out why we hadn't wanted them in our football practice. As soon as Michelle asked me if I wanted to play Ping-Pong, her little brothers decided that's exactly what they wanted to do, so we gave in and played doubles with them the rest of the afternoon.

When it got to be about dinnertime I was sure I'd really have to leave, but again Michelle surprised me. When she asked me if I wanted to stay to dinner, I told her I'd already eaten my share at her house, but if she wanted to come home with me I was sure there'd be enough. I was reasonably sure she had a date that night, but sure enough she came back to my house with me and was an instant hit with my parents and Chrissie. Particularly my sister, because from that moment on she modeled herself after Michelle—dressing like her. She thought Michelle was the greatest thing since computer games.

That night, my folks went out and Michelle and I and Chrissie sat around watching TV. Not that we were thrilled that my sister was with us, at least I wasn't, but Chrissie seemed determined not to let us out of her sight for an instant. Despite her presence, we had a great time, and when I walked her home later it seemed like we'd known each other forever. I didn't try to kiss her or anything that night— after all, it wasn't even a date—but she agreed to go to the football game with me the following Friday night, and that would really be a date.

From then on, Michelle and I were together probably half our waking hours. Until I got my driver's license we walked to school together every morning, and a lot of the time she watched me practice after school. I don't think a day went by that we didn't see each other and also talk on the phone, and we even ate over at each other's houses all the time. We were a couple, and if anyone had told me in those days that Michelle and I would eventually break up, I would have denied it and thought the person was crazy. She was funny and nice and affectionate, and I never got over thinking she was the prettiest girl I'd ever seen.

And yet, in spite of all that, it was over now, though I couldn't help hurting that it was only over for me and not for Michelle. I had never wanted to hurt her, but it seemed as if from the first moment I saw Sandy—well maybe not the first moment, I still thought she was a boy then—I was obsessed with her, and for no good reason at all Michelle just didn't seem important to me anymore. Maybe all the challenge had gone out of our relationship, I don't know. It had gotten so that I knew Michelle as well as myself, and maybe that wasn't so good. I can't pretend to know all the answers. All I knew was that I now felt like Michelle was an old friend, and all my romantic interests were focused on Sandy.

I decided before going to sleep that night that it would be a good idea for Michelle and me to talk in person. I thought I owed her an explanation, and I hadn't been happy with the way our phone conversation had ended that night. I figured if I talked to her in person, explained how I felt, she'd probably feel better about the whole thing.

The next morning I went over to Michelle's house. I hadn't counted on the kind of reception I received. Her parents and little brothers seemed so happy to see me I felt embarrassed. Her parents were polite enough not to ask where I'd been, but her brothers kept saying, "Hey, Tom, why don't you ever come over anymore?" Finally, Michelle appeared and she didn't look all that happy to see me. I told her I'd like to talk to her and we went out on her patio and sat down.

"What'd you want, Tom?" she asked me, getting right to the point without any small talk first.

"I was a little upset about your phone call last night," I told her.

"I was a little upset myself." I couldn't read anything from her face; she seemed to be in better control than she'd been on the phone.

"I'd really like to be friends with you, Michelle, if it's at all possible."

The look she gave me convinced me it wasn't possible. I waited for her to say something but she just sat there, her lips pressed into a thin line.

"I didn't mean this to happen, I swear. And the dumb part of it is, I think you're a lot better-looking than Sandy, and you're more fun to be with, too."

She gave me this incredulous look. "I'm more fun to be with but you preferring being with her?"

"I know it doesn't make any sense."

"Just what is it about her? She seems nice enough, but she's awfully young, isn't she?"

"Yeah, she's young, and I don't know what it is about her. It's something, though; she's really gotten to me."

Her body seemed to droop. "I guess you can't help who you fall in love with."

"Things would be a lot easier if you could."

She didn't say anything to that, just stared past me, her eyes beginning to look a little glazed.

"I was surprised you started seeing Mike Stern," I told her.

"Leave Mike out of this!"

"He just doesn't seem your type, that's all."

"Who's my type, *you*?"

"You could probably get any guy you wanted."

"Well, if it's any of your business, which it isn't, at the moment I want Mike."

"Yeah, well, I always thought he was a good guy."

She didn't say anything, just raised an eyebrow at that piece of news.

"You're probably a good influence on him."

"Don't pretend to care when you don't, Tom."

"I do care, Michelle—I'd really like us to be friends."

Michelle leaned back in her chair and eyed me speculatively. "You want to go to the movies this afternoon?"

"Michelle!"

"Well, that's what friends are for. What kind of friend did you want to be?"

I shrugged. "I just figured when we saw each other we ought to be friendly at least, you know?"

"In other words, you want me to make things easy for you."

"Come on, Michelle—"

"Don't 'come on' me, Tom. In fact I think you ought to go. I don't feel much like talking to you anymore."

"Michelle—"

"Get out of here!" She said that pretty loudly and I was afraid her family would hear, so I got up.

"Look, why don't we—"

"Just get out!"

She was practically yelling by that point so I headed around the side of her yard and went out the gate so I wouldn't have to see her folks again. I just don't understand why girls can't have nice friendly conversations without getting emotional. I thought if she'd been the one to break up with me, I'd have taken it a whole lot better. But girls—they have to get emotional about the least little thing. As I headed for home I was sure she was probably crying, crying and cursing me at the same time. I'd heard before that girls just won't let loose and I guess that's the truth.

Well, I'd tried, and that was all I could do. When I got home I called Sandy and asked her if she wanted to take in a movie, but she said she had too much studying to do. Then I tried calling Kenny, but his mother said he went somewhere with Billie. So I went downstairs and asked Chrissie if she wanted to go to the movies, but she had made plans to go with her friends. It turned out to be a pretty boring day; all I did was hang around the house.

The following weekend Sandy was going to New York again, this time to participate in the Mobil Track and Field Championships. She trained really hard that week. Her usual routine was to run all sorts of combinations. Sometimes this involved a series of sprints, some 440s, 220s, even some dashes followed by some middle-distance turns. Except for at practice I barely saw her that week, and whenever I tried calling her on the phone in the evening, she was always working out on her weights or other equipment and would only talk to me for about a minute. If I had let myself I could've become jealous of her obsession with track, but it only seemed natural to me. I mean if I were that good, I'd be obsessed, too.

Once again, the papers all carried pictures of her that week, but a lot of them were duplicates of the ones I already had on my wall, so I didn't cut them all out. The meet was on Thursday night and it wasn't televised, so early Friday morning I got up to read about it in the paper. When I went downstairs my dad was already at the breakfast table looking at the paper while he drank his second cup of coffee.

"Your friend was hurt, Tom," he said to me.

"Sandy?"

He nodded. "Not badly, but it looks as though she won't be running for a while."

I practically ripped the newspaper out of his hands. It seems that she was moving up on a girl who was a full lap behind her, and when it looked like the girl wasn't going to move over to let her pass, Sandy started passing on the inside, only at the last moment the girl moved and their legs got tangled up together and they both fell hard. It said that Sandy tried to get up and keep running but her ankle collapsed. Torn ligaments was the diagnosis.

I knew that wasn't something that wouldn't heal, but it would take a while, and she wouldn't be able to run again until she'd rested that ankle a good long time.

"That must've been a big disappointment to her," my father remarked, looking at me to see my reaction to the news.

"I think she's going to miss running more than she's going to worry about losing the race."

"Well, look at the bright side of things, Tom. You'll probably be able to see more of her now."

That had occurred to me the moment I read the article. I know it sounds selfish and nasty, but a small part of me couldn't help but be pleased that she'd be out of commission for a while. Now we'd be able to see each other like a normal couple, at least until her ankle healed.

Sandy wasn't in school that day, and after school I headed straight for the house.

"How is she?" I asked her mother when she let me in.

"Bored. Maybe you can cheer her up."

Sandy was on the couch in the living room, her ankle in an ace bandage, watching TV. She looked small and pale and very unhappy, but when she saw me her face broke into a smile.

"I'm so glad to see you, Tom," she said, and the way she said it I knew she really meant it. I sat down beside her and took her hand and got on with the business of cheering her up.

Chapter Seven

It was a few days into March before Sandy started using her ankle again. Up until then she stayed off it, hopping around on her other foot when she absolutely had to move from one room to the other. I offered to carry her a couple of times, but she reminded me she wasn't a helpless baby.

Her coach came over to see her regularly and told her he didn't want her even attempting to run again for a couple of months. When she protested, he told her he didn't want her to risk getting a permanent injury, and at that she meekly submitted. He patted me on the shoulder and told me to keep her in line, and I promised him that I would.

Her mom was taking a lot of time off from work, but when I'd show up she'd go to the office and leave the two of us alone. She seemed to like me and I guess she trusted me with Sandy.

During the time when she had to stay completely off her ankle, I did everything I could think of to keep her amused.

I brought games over and taught them to her, we studied together, and I helped her with everything but French, which I'd never taken. We also watched a lot of TV, more than I'd ever watched before, until it got so that I could barely stand the sight of it.

Sometimes I'd get Kenny and Billie over to her house and the four of us would play around with her weights or get into a game of Monopoly, which was Kenny's favorite game if you don't count Pac-Man, which I don't.

A lot of things changed between us during that time, and one of them was that Sandy started calling me on the phone a lot. Where before I don't think she had called me once, now she was calling me every night, sometimes more than once; we would talk for hours. And if for some reason I wasn't around, Chrissie said she talked to her. She came to rely on me a lot during that time, and if I was late coming over to see her after school she'd get a little upset.

Another crazy thing was that she got all this mail. I don't think she got one get-well card from anyone at school, but fans of hers all over the country were sending her cards and letters, and we'd sit around together and read them. She even answered a lot of them, just for something to do, and sometimes I helped her. A few guys wrote her letters that sounded like they were more interested in her as a girl than as a runner, and I wouldn't let her answer those. One guy even said he had a scrapbook of pictures of her, but I guess there are all kinds of nuts out there.

Then one day when I arrived at her door she answered it herself. When I yelled at her to get back on the couch, she just grinned and shook her head.

"The doctor said I could start walking around today," she told me, "just so long as I don't overdo it at first."

"You want to go for a ride?" I asked her.

"Oh, yes! It'd be so great to get out of here for a while."

I wanted to carry her out to my car, but she insisted on walking on her own. We took a long drive down Pacific Coast Highway, almost to Laguna Beach. At one point, I pulled off the highway and asked her if she wanted to walk along the beach.

"Walking in the sand will help to strengthen your ankle," I told her, which was something I'd read.

We held hands and walked a way, but when I could see she was starting to tire, I picked her up and this time insisted on carrying her back to the car. I don't know why she thought that was treating her like a baby; I thought it was kind of romantic, myself. She put her arms around my neck when I carried her, and every time I stopped to kiss her, she didn't protest at all but just kissed me back.

That night her mom called to say she was working late and I stayed at Sandy's and fixed her some dinner. Now this is pretty much of a joke as there's nothing much I can cook, but I can make superb grilled cheese sandwiches, and I managed to open a can of tomato soup and heat it, so that's what we had. It wasn't exactly a major deviation from our health diets, but came pretty close.

During lunch in the cafeteria one day, Kenny said to me, "When are you going to stop devoting all your time to Sandy and start devoting some to your friends?"

"You mean you?" I asked him, kind of surprised at his remark.

"Well, I can't say I've exactly seen much of you lately."

"I've had to be with Sandy, you know that."

"*Had* to be?"

"She doesn't have anyone else, Kenny."

"That's her problem, not yours."

"Come on, wouldn't you do the same for Billie?"

"I don't think I'd spend all my time with her, but then I'm not the martyr type."

"But I *want* to spend all my time with her."

"We used to have some good times together, man, you remember?"

"I still see you at school."

"You hardly even come to practice anymore. Some of the guys are wondering if you're still on the team."

"I need to drive Sandy home after school, you know that."

"Why can't her mother do that?"

"Because I offered to do it. I think I might drop track anyway; it really doesn't interest me that much anymore."

"Are you kidding, man?"

I hadn't really thought about it before, but track did take up a lot of time and it wasn't as though I were going to seriously pursue it in college. "I'm perfectly serious," I told him, "in fact I think I'll talk to Zabo about it today."

"Come on, Tom, don't do something you'll regret later."

"I don't think I'll regret it."

"Oh, man—I think you're sick."

"It's not as though I'm looking to get a track scholarship or anything. UCLA's already accepted me, and anyway, I don't think I'll run for them next year. I'll probably just concentrate on my studies."

"You'll probably just concentrate on driving down here all the time to see Sandy."

"What's the matter with that? Don't you plan on seeing Billie anymore when you get in college?"

"Billie and I both know we're not going to see each other forever. We've talked about it. We both plan on dating other people next year, it only makes sense."

"Then I guess you don't really love her," I said, making a judgment.

"I'm only a kid, man, what do I know about love?" he said as a joke, but I didn't think it was funny.

"Lots of guys our age get married," I informed him.

"Yeah, crazy guys. Come on, man, these are high-school girlfriends, that's all. I can't even believe you're talking like this. I thought I knew you, but I guess I was wrong."

"You just don't understand, Kenny—we're in love."

"She's told you she loves you?"

"Not in so many words."

"That's what I figured."

"You think you know everything, Kenny, but you're wrong about this. She loves me, I know she does."

"Yeah, well I hope you two are real happy together."

"What's that supposed to mean?"

"Well, you've dropped all your friends, I guess she's all you have left."

"I haven't dropped anyone; I've just been busy lately."

Kenny just shrugged and looked away from me. "Sometimes I wish you were still going with Michelle. You were a lot easier to take then, believe me."

"Well, you know, you don't have to *take* me, Kenny."

"That's what I'm thinking."

I couldn't believe this was happening; it was like the scene with Michelle. Kenny'd been my best friend for years and it was hard to believe that our friendship was threatened over something as silly as this.

"Listen, Kenny," I said, getting up, "I'll give you a call tonight. We'll talk."

"Yeah, you do that, man."

As it turned out I didn't have a chance to call him that night, and when I looked for him in the cafeteria the next day, he wasn't around. That same day I talked to the coach after school about dropping off the track team.

"I thought you already had quit," Zabo told me, no warmth in his voice at all.

"I've been helping out Sandy," I told him.

"Yeah, so I've heard."

"I figure it's more important, Zabo. I mean, I'm never going to amount to much as far as track goes, but she's a star. I'm helping her get back in shape, you know?"

"You're a good runner, Tom, I hate to see you just drop it like this. Sandy would be the first to understand. I don't think she'd want you giving it up."

"It's my decision, Zabo, and I'm going to stick by it."

He didn't even shake my hand or anything, just nodded at me when I left. I was feeling pretty good about the whole thing. I felt like I was giving something up for Sandy, proving my love for her. In fact I could hardly wait to get over to her house and tell her.

She met me at the door and we went straight in to her workout room. As I was massaging her ankle for her, I said, "Guess what I did today?"

"Flunked your Spanish test?"

"No, I passed that, but just barely."

"Okay, what'd you do?"

"Quit the track team."

She didn't even seem very surprised. "Good, then we'll have more time together."

"I just didn't think it was all that important."

"Won't you miss it?"

"Maybe, but it's not as though I'm really good, like you."

She just nodded, which kind of annoyed me.

"Would you be so interested in it if you weren't so good?" I asked her.

"I don't think so. You know, I've never been beaten in a race. I don't know how I'd feel if someone else beat me."

I kind of chuckled even though I wasn't amused. "It's bound to happen some day, you know."

"Why?"

"It just is, that's all. One day someone else will come along who's even better, and that'll be it."

"Maybe, but by that time I'll probably be so old I won't even care."

I hoped for her sake that this was true. I had a feeling Sandy wouldn't take well to being number two instead of number one.

I finished massaging her ankle and we took turns lifting weights. She was a slim girl and you never noticed her muscles ordinarily, but when we'd finish pumping iron we'd compare muscles and hers weren't bad at all. Not as large as mine, but then she was only a girl.

After that, I put some music on her stereo and we did a bunch of situps and she taught me some yoga she'd learned. I found that stuff a little hard to do, but Sandy could even stand on her head in the middle of the floor without holding on to anything, and I was determined to get to the point where I could do it, too.

When she was ending the session by standing on her head, I got down next to her on the floor and stared at her upside down. "You look silly like that," I told her.

"You're just jealous because you can't do it."

"Oh, is that right?" I asked, starting to tickle her in the ribs. I knew by then how ticklish she was and used this knowledge on occasion to my own advantage.

"Stop that this minute, Tom!"

But something in me wouldn't let me stop, and soon I had her laughing so hard she couldn't maintain her balance and tumbled down beside me on the floor. Her face was red from all the blood rushing to her head, and she looked so cute and flushed I just had to kiss her. As usual, she didn't bother closing her eyes when we kissed and by that time I was used to keeping my own open. It was kind of fun to be able to watch the expressions on her face.

"All you ever want to do is kiss," she told me in a teasing way, rolling away from me on the floor.

"That's because I'm a normal red-blooded American boy."

"I think it's because you're weird!"

"Weird? You think kissing is *weird*?"

"I don't think it's any big deal."

"Then obviously I'm doing something wrong," I told her, grabbing her again and giving her another kiss. This time I really concentrated on it and tried to make it memorable. But when I finally came up for air she just laughed.

"Still weird, huh?" I asked.

"It's okay, I just don't know why you always want to do it."

"That's what you're supposed to do with your girlfriend," I informed her.

"Am I your girlfriend?"

"Well, what would you call it?"

She seemed to ponder that. "I guess I don't really know what you do with a boyfriend because I've never had one before."

"And do you like having one?" I always seemed to need reassurance from her since she never offered any on her own.

"It's nice having someone to work out with."

"Is that all?" I persisted.

"It's nice having you around."

"How come you don't have any friends?"

She sat up in the lotus position and I tried to do the same, but my knees just wouldn't touch the floor like hers did. "I just don't have time for them. Anyway, most of the girls think I'm crazy for being so interested in track."

"There're lots of girls going out for track these days."

"What do I need friends for? I have you."

Well, I couldn't argue with that. Anyway, it was beginning to look as though I was in the same boat. I hardly saw anything of Kenny anymore, and when I did he wasn't very friendly. I don't know, maybe I'd just outgrown him. I think that sometimes happens when you get serious about a girl for the first time.

That day I took her over to my house for dinner. Sandy was still shy around my family but they seemed to like her, although my mother treated her as if she was younger than Chrissie. My sister seemed to have some reservations about her, but then she'd been so crazy about Michelle it didn't surprise me. I think Chrissie thought that one day Michelle and I would get back together and everything would be normal again. At least her idea of normal.

It's strange, but Sandy changed in a lot of ways during this time. First of all, she was putting on some weight from not running. This didn't seem to worry her because she said as soon as she started running again she'd take it off, but I wasn't so sure. The less body fat you carry the faster you can run, and I didn't think she knew how hard it was to take off weight since she'd probably never had any excess weight before. But with an added fifteen pounds I thought she looked a lot prettier. She filled out, looked more like a girl. I wouldn't take her for a boy running around the track anymore.

But even more than physically, she seemed to be changing mentally. She wasn't nearly as shy anymore and she seemed to make up for her lack of running by doing a lot of talking. I had thought she was really quiet when I first knew her, but now I could hardly shut her up. And she developed a curiosity about all kinds of things she'd never shown an interest in before. One thing was television, and I don't think that was such a good thing. Before the accident, she had rarely watched it because she never had the time. But since

her accident I could never get her to shut it off. She knew
nearly every show on in the evenings and if she missed one
for some reason she got upset.

Another thing she took up was painting. At the beginning when she couldn't walk around, her mother had
brought her home some watercolors, brushes and pads of
paper. At first I thought she was only fooling around with
them, but then I noticed she had a real talent for drawing.
One night, when we were sitting around her living room, she
drew a picture of me that even I recognized. For a while, she
drew better than she painted, but soon her pictures were
looking really good and whenever she watched television,
she also painted.

This newly found interest in art prompted me to drive her
down to Laguna Beach one Saturday to visit the galleries,
and she was so pleased by that excursion that the next Saturday I took her up to Los Angeles to the Museum of Art
there. She seemed lost in a world of her own as we wan-
dered through the place, and it occurred to me that it was
probably good that she was developing interests other than
running. She wouldn't be running forever, and it's good to
have more than one interest in life.

One day, for no reason at all, I remembered that Michelle's mother was an artist. Her husband had even converted her garage into a studio for her, and I heard she gave
lessons there. On an impulse, I told Sandy about it, and
asked her if she'd be interested in taking lessons.

"I'd love to," she told me. "I know I can draw, but I still
don't know how to get some of the techniques with watercolors that real artists get."

She was so excited about it that then and there I called
Michelle's mother on the phone.

"Michelle's not home, Tom," she told me.

"Actually, it was you I wanted to speak to," I said. "A friend of mine is interested in taking painting lessons," and then I told her a little bit about Sandy. It ended with her asking us to come by and talk to her, but first I made sure that Michelle wasn't home.

Sandy and Michelle's mother hit it off, and it was decided that Sandy would attend her Saturday morning class. The whole time we were talking to her Michelle's mom was looking from me to Sandy with a quizzical look, but I figured Michelle would fill her in later. At least it didn't seem like her mother held it against me for breaking up with Michelle. Who knows, maybe she was even glad? I think both our sets of parents thought we were getting a little too serious when we were going together.

I have to admit I wasn't thinking about Michelle in all of this, so I wasn't prepared when she cornered me in the hallway at school the next day. She didn't look so good, either. While Sandy was putting on weight, Michelle was taking it off, and she was getting so skinny I'm not sure I would've looked at her twice if I had just met her. She didn't seem to care about her appearance at all anymore; it used to be that that was one of her major concerns.

"I really can't believe what a despicable character you've turned out to be, Tom Cunningham," she said to me first thing.

"What's your problem now, Michelle?" I was determined to be civilized with her at all costs.

"I can't believe you got *my* mother to teach *your* girlfriend painting. Are you purposely going out of your way to annoy me or are you just so inconsiderate you don't even think first?"

"What's the big deal, Michelle—your mother teaches painting and Sandy wanted a teacher. I should think you'd be glad to see your mom get another student."

Her hands went on her hips and her eyes blazed fire. "Is that what you really think, Tom? Are you really that stupid?"

"Get off my back, Michelle."

"Just do me a favor, will you, Tom? For the short time you have left in this school, will you please just pretend you don't even know me? Because I sure wish to heaven I'd never known you!"

She was talking loudly and a crowd had gathered around to listen. When she turned and stalked off, I looked around and kind of shrugged, trying to laugh it off, but the kids just avoided my eyes and walked away. I think I even saw Kenny in the crowd, but he disappeared before I could say anything to him.

I told Sandy about the encounter after school, thinking we could laugh together over Michelle's outrageous behavior. She didn't laugh, though. She just shrugged and said, "I don't know why she should be mad at *me*; *I* didn't tell you to break up with her."

I suppose she had a point, but nonetheless I had broken up with Michelle directly because of her. I didn't think it would be a good idea to point this fact out to her, though. "Aren't you glad I did?" I asked.

She looked over at me in her new, teasing manner. "I suppose so."

I feigned indignance. "You *suppose* so? Where do you think you'd be now if you hadn't met me?"

She chuckled. "Riding home in my mother's car."

"Right! And wouldn't you rather be riding with me?"

She gave a nonchalant shrug and looked out the window.

"I asked you a question, Sandy."

"I'm thinking about it."

"Who would have amused you those long hours when you weren't allowed to walk?"

"My mother probably would've hired someone to stay with me."

"Yeah, some old lady who would've watched the soaps."

"Oh, I don't know. Maybe she would've hired some good-looking young guy who wouldn't always treat me like a child."

I slammed on the brakes and pulled over the curb. "Do I treat you like a child?"

She started to laugh. "Sometimes."

"Name just once!"

"Well, you were always trying to carry me around at first. You remember."

"And you think that's treating you like a child?"

She nodded.

"Well for your information, Sandy, sometimes a boy likes to carry a girl. Did you ever think of that?"

That made her laugh all the harder. "Well, for your information, Tom, we girls want to be treated like equals these days, or hadn't you heard that news?"

"You know, Sandy, you're the least romantic person I've ever known."

"Is that bad?"

"Sometimes it is."

"Was Michelle romantic?"

I was pretty startled to hear her ask that. She'd never before referred to my going with Michelle, and I had a hope that at last she was showing some jealousy. It would be the first time, I'll tell you that. I'd tried on occasion to get some spark of jealousy out of her, but I'd always failed.

"Yeah, Michelle was very romantic. Most girls are."

"I'd say most boys are."

"Well, you'd be wrong. That just shows you don't know very much about boys yet."

"I know you, and you're romantic. Or aren't you a normal boy?"

It's pretty hard to answer a loaded question like that. I consider myself normal, but I guess I am something of a romantic. So I just didn't answer it at all, just pulled out again into the street and continued in silence to her house. I knew she was watching me, waiting for some answer, but I just couldn't think of a good one and finally the silence stretched for so long any answer I came up with would have sounded silly.

We got to her house and went inside. I waited until she was lifting weights, and then I asked her, "Why did you ask me that about Michelle? Are you jealous of her?" Dumb question, I know, but I was always asking Sandy dumb questions it seemed.

"Why should I be jealous of her?"

Good question; much better than mine had been. "Most girls would be," I said. I know when I first started going with Michelle I was jealous of every guy she'd ever gone out with. Which was one advantage of going with someone like Sandy, who'd never dated before.

"No reason," I told her.

"Then why did you ask? Why should I be jealous of her? You picked me over her, didn't you?"

"It doesn't bother you that I went with her before you?"

"That'd be pretty silly—I didn't even know you then."

"That's what I mean, you're not romantic."

She sat up on the exercise bench and glared at me. "I don't need to be; you're romantic enough for the two of us!"

I loved it when she showed a temper because it was so rare. She looked so cute glaring at me that I had to grab her and give her a big kiss. It started out to be playful, but soon I had my arms wrapped around her and we were seriously kissing. When we were through kissing, I just hugged her to me. Then, out of nowhere, because I certainly hadn't planned it, I said, "I love you, Sandy."

I waited, and when she didn't say anything I thought maybe she hadn't heard what I'd said. "I really do, you know; I really love you," I told her, saying it kind of softly in her ear the way Michelle used to like.

"I'm glad," she finally said.

Those weren't exactly the words I was waiting to hear. "That's all you can say is you're glad?" I asked, pushing her away from me.

"What do you want me to say, I'm *not* glad?"

"I'd like to hear how you feel about me, that's what!"

She leaned back on the exercise bench again and began lifting the weights.

"Could you just tell me that, is that too much to ask? I mean, I just told you I loved you, can't you say anything better than you're glad?"

"What're you getting upset about, Tom?"

"This is just what I mean, you don't have a romantic bone in your body."

"I don't know how to say things like that. I've never said anything like that to a boy."

Well, I didn't think that was much of an excuse, and I was pretty angry by then, so I just walked out of the room and went to the kitchen and got myself a glass of water. But then I began thinking about it, and remembering how hard it had been for me to tell Michelle the first time. I mean, I planned it weeks in advance, and then when the moment came I could barely get the words out. It's really hard the first time you tell a girl you love her. I guess I just kept forgetting how young and inexperienced Sandy really was.

When I got back to the room Sandy was on the exercycle. I stood in the doorway looking at her, and she finally saw me and looked over. "You still mad at me?" she asked.

"No, I'm not mad at you. I just wish there was more reciprocity in this relationship, that's all."

"You talk funny, you know that?"

"That's just something I heard my father say once. It means, in simple terms, if I tell you I love you, I guess I expect to hear the same thing from you."

"I love you," she said in about the same tone of voice she'd use to say she loved a movie. Still, she'd finally said it.

"Get off that bike and tell me," I ordered her.

Like a good little girl, she got off the bike and walked over to me, putting her arms around my waist and resting her face against my chest. "I love you, Tom," she said, and it seemed to me they were the most beautiful words I'd ever heard.

Chapter Eight

I knew Sandy's birthday was in April because the magazine article about her had said when she was born. Not that she ever mentioned the fact, but that was okay with me as I planned on having a surprise birthday party for her at my house.

I told Sandy's mother about it swearing her to secrecy. She said Sandy would love it, that she hadn't had a real birthday party in years. That seemed kind of sad to me; all the kids I know still get birthday parties. Mine would be the following month.

There turned out to be one big problem: Sandy didn't have any friends to invite. And I'd kind of lost contact with mine.

I told my mother about it and she said she'd bake Sandy a chocolate birthday cake and get in plenty of food and stuff to drink, and Chrissie even offered to decorate the family room with streamers and balloons and such. But the big problem still was who to invite.

I started off by stopping Billie in the hall one day and telling her about the party and asking her if she'd mind inviting some of the kids from the track team.

"Why don't you ask them yourself?" she asked me.

"Well, you know, since I dropped off the team..."

"They're still your friends, you know, Tom."

I wasn't so sure about that, even Kenny barely greeted me when I saw him around these days. Billie's really nice, though, and she finally said she'd ask them for me.

After that, I expected some of the kids to stop me in the halls and say they were coming, but no one did. About a week before the party I started getting nervous that maybe no one would come. So I drove over to Garden Grove one day and asked Sandy's coach if he'd tell the members of the team about the party, emphasizing that it was going to be a surprise for Sandy.

He said he was sure they'd be glad to come, and I wrote down my address and phone number for him to give to them. I thought it would really be a good surprise for Sandy when all those kids showed up, since she hadn't seen them in so long.

I couldn't decide what to get Sandy for her birthday. I wanted it to be something personal, like jewelry, so that she'd think of me every time she wore it. I didn't have much money, but I finally found something I could afford that I thought was perfect. It was a sterling-silver running shoe. The clerk in the store said it was for a charm bracelet, but I knew she didn't have one, so instead I got her a thin chain to wear it on. I would have liked to have some message engraved on the bottom of it, but it was too small for that.

The party was set for eight o'clock. I figured I'd pick up Sandy about quarter of, then by the time we got back to my house all the kids could be hiding and jump out and yell "Happy Birthday" when we came in. Corny, I know, but what else do you do at a surprise party?

I had told Sandy we were going to the movies that night. When I picked her up her mother gave me a wink behind Sandy's back that almost made me laugh out loud. The fact that Sandy didn't have any other friends had made it easy to keep the party a surprise from her and I knew she didn't have a clue.

She did notice that I was driving in the wrong direction for the movie, so I told her I'd left my wallet at home and had to go back and pick it up.

"I've got money with me," she said, but I told her I shouldn't be driving without my license and that it was in my wallet, too.

When I got to my house I didn't see any cars parked out front and figured the kids had parked a little distance away. Sandy looked like she was going to wait in the car with me, but I told her there was something in the house I wanted to show her, so she got out and walked up to the door with me. Chrissie grabbed me as soon as we got in the house and pulled me over to one side so that Sandy couldn't hear.

"No one's here yet, Tom," she whispered.

Great! All that planning, and the kids, as usual, were all going to be late. I guess I should have figured on that to begin with. No one ever arrives on time to a party.

We were here now, though, and it would look pretty suspicious to Sandy if I were to drive off with her and then invent another excuse to return home.

She was already looking suspicious, her glance going from Chrissie's face to my own. "What did you want to show me?' she asked, and I kind of shrugged at Chrissie, then took Sandy's hand and led her into the family room.

Chrissie had done such a good job that it looked professional. Dozens of red and white balloons hung from the ceiling and red and white streamers, wound around one another, decorated all the walls. In the place of honor on the table was the big cake my mom had made with "Happy Birthday Sandy" written on it along with fifteen red candles, and there was enough food spread out to feed half the school.

I looked over to see Sandy's reaction and she was biting her lip and looking like she might burst into tears. "Happy birthday," I said to her, putting my arm around her shoulders.

My parents came into the room and wished her a happy birthday, as did Chrissie, and then I explained to her that there were people coming who supposedly were to jump out from behind the furniture and surprise her, only we'd arrived there too early and none of them had arrived yet.

"It doesn't matter," she said, leaning against me. "You're here, that's all that matters."

Well, that was nice to hear, but one person hardly constitutes a birthday party. I felt like getting on the phone to a few of them and telling them to hurry over, but then I realized that I didn't even know who was coming.

"Who did you invite?" Sandy was asking me, just as though she could read my mind.

"Some of our track team, and I also had your coach at Runners West invite the athletes over there."

Sandy was looking puzzled. "But why would they come to a party for me? I don't even know most of them."

"They know who you are," I said.

"Maybe, but I've never even said a word to most of them. If I hadn't gotten well-known they wouldn't even know who I was."

"I figured you'd have some friends over there."

She shook her head. "They're all older than me; they've always treated me like a little kid."

"We don't need them anyway," my mother said, trying to help out. "There'll be enough of Tom's friends coming to make it a good party."

I was glad she thought so; as for me, I wasn't so sure. The team could easily be mad at me for quitting, and I figured I'd be lucky if Billie and Kenny showed up.

For something to do, and because the room seemed so quiet for a party, I went over to the stereo and put on some records. While I was doing this I saw that my mom was lighting the candles on the cake. My first reaction was to tell her to wait until the others got there, but then I was afraid maybe there wouldn't be any others, so I didn't say anything.

My family made a big fuss over Sandy blowing out the candles and making a wish, and then Chrissie asked her what she'd wished for, and before I could say anything about wishes not coming true if you tell, Sandy was telling everyone she'd wished for her ankle to heal quickly so that she could run again.

Every other girl in the world would make some kind of a romantic wish, maybe about getting or keeping a boyfriend, but not Sandy. Her ankle was coming along nicely anyway, so I didn't see why she had to waste a perfectly good wish on it.

I went to my room to get her present, and when I got back everyone was sitting around eating cake and ice cream. I sat down at the table and handed Sandy her present.

"You shouldn't have done this," she said, "the party was more than enough."

"It's nothing much," I told her, waiting anxiously while she carefully took off the ribbon and paper and then lifted out the silver shoe. Her eyes lit up when she saw it was a running shoe, and then she handed it to me and lowered her head so that I could put it around her neck. My parents were suitably impressed by my good taste in gifts, but they might also have been remembering the time they saw me hang a silver heart around Michelle's neck.

"Oh, Tom, I love it," said Sandy, and I would have liked to give her a birthday kiss then and there but I figured we didn't need an audience around for that.

After that we sat around and ate our cake and tried to make conversation, but the party was a real bust. If I had meant it to be just family it would've been okay, but you could see by the amount of food and cans of drinks that a lot of people were expected. I was feeling more and more depressed by the minute, when finally the doorbell rang and I hurried off to answer it.

It was Kenny and Billie, and I'd never been so happy to see anyone in my life. "Did you ask the other kids?" I asked Billie as soon as they got in the door.

"Sure I did," she assured me, "but we had a meet today and got back late. They'll be along."

If I'd kept up at all with what was happening around school I would've known about the meet, and I was embarrassed that they could see that I hadn't known.

"I really appreciate your coming," I said to Kenny.

"I didn't come for you, man, I came for Sandy," he said, obviously still angry at me for what he felt was my desertion.

I took them into the family room where Kenny gave Sandy a birthday kiss, as did Billie, and then Kenny spied all the food and started to dig right in. My parents and Chrissie left then and while it still didn't seem like much of a party, we at least had Kenny and Billie to talk to, and Sandy seemed to enjoy listening to them talk about the meet that day. It was the first time in a while that Sandy had had a chance to talk about running, and I could see from the expression on her face that while she didn't complain, she was really missing it.

As for myself, I really didn't want to hear about it. Every time Kenny started talking about some event, I knew he was thinking I was a traitor who'd deserted the team. I found that I wasn't missing it at all. I was probably getting somewhat out of shape, but as soon as Sandy was okay I'd start to do some running with her along with the other stuff we worked out at.

A little later, Ann Harris and three of the other girls from the team showed up. They'd gone together and bought Sandy a T-shirt that said Keep Running on it that I could tell she liked. And that was it as far as the party went; no one else showed up. Since there were six girls and only two guys, Kenny was kept busy dancing with all the girls, and I spent most of the time trying to get everyone to eat more food so we wouldn't have to throw out so much when the party was over.

Sandy seemed to be having a good time; I guess she enjoyed it more with just a few people as she'd never liked crowds. I kept thinking back to last year when Michelle threw a big birthday party for me and half the school had showed up. Everyone had said it was the best party of the year, and I'd been hoping Sandy's would turn out like that. My birthday was only a few weeks away, but I was starting to hint I wouldn't have a party this year. Anyway, birthday parties are for kids and I was almost in college.

Kenny was pretty cool to me for most of the evening. Oh, he was polite and all, but he didn't kid around with me the way he used to. At one point, though, he seemed to warm up, and he told me that he was getting a job that summer as a lifeguard in Lake Arrowhead, which is this great resort up in the mountains.

"You could probably get one too if you applied now," he told me.

"I don't know, Kenny."

"Listen, man, it's good pay and we'd get to spend the summer in Arrowhead! You can't beat that, can you?"

I'd always loved Lake Arrowhead; last summer, it would have sounded like a dream come true. Plus, I'd be able to save some money for college. But going to Arrowhead would mean leaving Sandy, and I figured I should be around to help train with her. We'd been together so much lately that I felt she'd be lost without me.

"I don't think so, Kenny, but thanks all the same."

"Well, think about it at least, okay? You have to apply this week if you want to get it."

"Yeah, I'll think about it."

"Promise?"

"Promise."

"You're not going to do it, are you? You're so hung up on that little girl you're afraid to leave town."

"What're you talking about, Kenny? I'm going to college in the fall, that's leaving her, isn't it?"

"The way you're going you'll probably stay at home and go to Long Beach State."

"Never. Not if I want to get into med school."

"Lots of girls up there, Tom—and you know how girls love lifeguards."

"Is that why you're going?"

"Who, me?" He gave me his innocent look. "I'm going for the money, that's all."

Billie and Sandy had walked up to us on the tail end of the conversation. Billie was chuckling when she said, "*Kenny* interested in *girls*? Why, you know Kenny'll be true to me up there at Arrowhead."

"Sure he will," I said with a grin.

"What's this about Arrowhead?" asked Sandy.

Kenny explained the situation to her and she looked at me and said, "Why don't you go? It sounds great."

"You wouldn't mind if I went?"

"I think you should do whatever you want to do."

I thought so too, and what I wanted to do was spend the summer with her. "I'm thinking about it," I told her, wishing she'd beg me to stay.

"My mom and I got a cabin up there one summer and we loved it," she said.

"Maybe you could do the same this summer," I suggested, but she just shook her head.

"No, not this summer."

At about eleven, the four girls took off, leaving the four of us alone. Things seemed to be getting a little boring, so I suggested a game of Monopoly, and since only Billie groaned at the suggestion, and that was mostly because Kenny plays a cutthroat game, I got out the board and we all sat down at the table. After the game, Kenny and Billie left, and Sandy helped me clean up the room before I took her home.

She kept saying what a good party it'd been and how much fun she'd had, which made me feel a little better, although my opinion was that it'd been a lousy party. But at least it had made her happy, and that'd been the whole point of it. I just wished more people had come; maybe I should have invited them in person.

When I walked her to the door I started apologizing about the party, but she turned around and put her hand over my lips. "Stop it, Tom—it was a wonderful party. That's the nicest thing anyone's ever done for me."

"You really liked it?" Me needing constant reassurance again.

"I loved it, and I love you for doing it for me."

I took her in my arms and pulled her close. "Is that the only reason you love me?"

"Don't talk silly, I've told you I loved you before."

"Yeah, but sometimes a guy likes to hear it again. You know, just so he knows it's still on."

She looked up at me, her expression serious. "I love you, Tom."

"Why? Because I love you?" I couldn't seem to stop asking her questions, even though sometimes I was afraid to hear the answer. The thing about Sandy is that she always spoke the truth, and that's not always easy to take.

"That's part of the reason."

"What's the rest?"

"Because you're nice to me."

I moved a little back from her. "You mean you'd love any guy who was nice to you?"

Her hands fell to her sides. "Oh, Tom, why do you always have to dissect everything I say? You're nice to me and you love me and that's made me love you back. What do you want to be loved for?"

I shrugged, unsure myself of the answer. "For me, I guess. For the person I am."

"Well, the person you are is very nice and loves me."

"I don't know, Sandy, I never know what you're really thinking about me. I don't know whether you like the way I look or the way I act or whether you're ever bored with me.... You never ask me what I think about or what I dream about and you practically never ask a personal question. Sometimes I think you take more interest in those characters on TV than you do in me."

Her eyes looked enormous in her small face. "I don't understand what you want from me, Tom."

"I think about you all the time, Sandy—do you ever think of me?"

"Of course I think of you. I call you up, don't I?"

"Okay, maybe you miss me, or maybe you're just bored, but do you ever spend any time just thinking about me?"

She was silent for a moment. "What time? I'm with you all the time."

"What about when you're in bed at night? Do you ever think about me then?"

She shook her head as though she didn't understand what I was saying. "I'm sleeping then."

"Okay, Sandy, forget it," I said with a sigh. "It's not important. What's important is that you had a happy birthday. Come here, now and give me a kiss."

She moved into my arms and we kissed for several minutes until she moved away at last and opened the door. "Thanks, Tom, I really loved it," she told me before going into the house.

I drove around for a while that night before going home. I thought back to what a puzzle I'd found Sandy when I first met her, and the problem was, she was still a puzzle to me. I might be going with her now and in love with her, but I still didn't feel like I knew her any better than I had in the beginning.

It hadn't been like that with Michelle. I got to know practically everything about her in a very short period of time, and she knew just as much about me. And Michelle had always been questioning me, wanting to know what I was feeling, asking me what had happened in my classes, discussing the lives of our different friends. I knew all about her family and what she'd done before she'd met me and what she wanted to do in the future. I had felt a tie to Michelle that I didn't feel with Sandy. And yet at the same time I was feeling far more emotions with Sandy than I had ever felt before. I don't know what it was she thought about when we were apart, but I sure knew what I thought about.

Her. I thought about her just about all the time. I figured I'd get over that after going with her for a while, but it didn't seem to be happening.

Well, maybe that's what kept relationships interesting. Maybe Michelle and I got too close too fast and it was bound to burn out. I'd just have to give Sandy time, that was all. I sure didn't want to do anything that would make *our* relationship burn out quick.

It was a good month, April. In a way, my wish was coming true. I wanted to spend all my time with Sandy and that month we were practically inseparable. We went to school together. She'd given me her schedule of classes so that I could arrange to see her in the halls during school hours. And after school we usually went over to her house and worked out and just fooled around. Nights we had to study, but every night we talked on the phone.

Weekends we did all sorts of things. Sometimes we would just take off in my car and drive wherever the impulse took us. One time, we went all the way down to the border of Mexico and back, and another, we took the boat over to Catalina Island and spent the day wondering around. I even got her up to Chavez Ravine to see one of the Dodger games, but she didn't like baseball much. We had fun, though, and when I clued her in to the finer points of the game, she caught on quickly. She said she found baseball too slow, though; I guess the ball players didn't run fast enough to suit her.

I never went to see about the summer job as a lifeguard. Kenny saw me in the hall one day at school and reminded me, but I really wasn't interested. Being away from Sandy for three months wasn't my idea of a great summer. Anyway, I'd already promised Sandy I'd teach her how to surf.

The last day of April fell on a Sunday, and when I asked Sandy what she wanted to do that day, she said she wanted to go to the beach. Well, the weather was nice, but it wasn't exactly beach weather, but she said she just wanted to sit around and have a picnic and talk. That sounded pretty good to me, so I got my mom to pack us a picnic lunch and I picked her up around noon when the fog had burned off.

We drove down to Corona del Mar, which has the prettiest beach in the area. We had the place almost to ourselves; there were a couple of guys throwing a football around, but that was all. I was already starving by the time we got there so we unpacked the lunch and dug in. Afterward, we stretched out on the sand and talked for a while, then Sandy challenged me to a race.

"No you don't," I cautioned her. "Not until the doctor says it's okay."

She just gave me this impish smile and got to her feet. "Come on, Tom, or I'll start without you."

I reached out to grab hold of her and pull her back down on the sand, but she jumped out of my reach. "Behave yourself, Sandy," I told her.

That seemed to be all she needed to defy me. She took off down the beach, and to stop her from hurting herself I took off after her. And the surprising thing was, I actually caught up with her, and when I did I tackled her and we both landed face down on the sand.

She turned around and glared at me. "Why did you do that?"

"Because I don't want you hurting yourself," I said, then realized I could have hurt her by tackling her. She seemed okay, though, as she sat up and crossed her legs.

"I have a surprise for you, Tom."

"I have a surprise for *you*—I ran faster than you did!"

The smile on her face faded. "You did, didn't you? What am I going to do, Tom, I've lost my speed."

"Your ankle's not ready yet, that's all."

"But that's my surprise—my doctor said I could start running again." Even as she said it her face lit up.

"That's fantastic," I told her, but I knew I wasn't feeling nearly as good about it as she was.

"But you could've beaten me!" she wailed.

"It's all that weight you've put on. You'll soon take it off."

"You said you liked it."

"Well, yeah, I think you look great, but you don't look as much like a runner anymore."

She wrinkled her nose and turned the corners of her mouth down. "I shouldn't have eaten that lunch."

I got up and reached down for her hand. "Well, come on, we'll run it off."

She was on her feet in an instant and running down the beach, with me following her.

"I'm running, I'm running," she shouted to the wind, and even as I watched, her style seemed to improve until she was almost the runner she was before. And that was after two months of not running!

After about a mile she slowed down and then came to a stop. I came up to where she was standing, out of breath, and just stood there watching her exultant smile. "Oh, Tom, I'm so happy. I'm running again, and I've never felt so good in my entire life!"

"You're really happy, aren't you?"

"Oh, yes!" And her face held a look of such pure happiness, such as I had never seen before, that it was almost blinding. And that happiness had nothing whatsoever to do with me.

Chapter Nine

May was all downhill.

I knew things would change when Sandy got back to running, but I guess I was kidding myself when I thought the two of us would go on the same way as we'd been going. I tried to think of those past two months as happy interludes, the exception rather than the norm, but even though I understood the changes, I fought them and hated them.

Things didn't happen all at once, though; it was a gradual process. That first week in May, I still drove Sandy to school and still managed to see her a few times during the day. After school, I drove her over to Runners West; she got a great welcome back from Coach Jenkins. He had drawn up a new running program for her to get her slowly back into shape, and while they went this together, I just stood to one side and watched the other runners working out. I didn't plan on working out with them myself and wasn't even dressed for it. Getting Sandy, not me, back into shape was my first priority.

When Sandy trotted out on the track, turning to wave to me before she began running, the coach turned to me. "What happened to you, Cunningham? I haven't seen you at any meets lately."

I kept my eyes on Sandy as I answered him, telling him I just didn't have the time anymore and wasn't planning to go out for track in college, anyway.

"Sorry to hear that," he said. "You were good, you know."

"Not that good," I said, nodding in Sandy's direction.

"Yeah, but you'll never have to compete against her."

He turned away and I took out my stopwatch. I was planning on timing Sandy, giving her the results as we drove home and then talking over with her ways in which she could get back her speed. I waited until she passed in front me for the first time, then let the watch run.

I let her get around twice, noting that her speed was way down and also noting that for some reason she was keeping her arms farther away from her body than she used to. Her form was off and I thought I ought to mention it to her, so when she came around for a third time, I yelled out, "Keep those elbows in, Sandy."

"What do you think you're doing?" Coach Jenkins asked me, coming over to me in a hurry.

"It's her arms," I explained to him. "She isn't holding them the way she used to."

"Don't you think I can see that?"

"I just thought she ought to know, that's all."

"Let me do the coaching here, okay, Cunningham?"

I made what I hoped was an indifferent shrug. Why was he on my case? I was only trying to help her.

"And what're you doing with that stopwatch?"

"I thought I'd time her."

"Look, kid, I think it'd be better if you stayed away while she works out. You're a distraction, you know?"

"Look, coach, I promise—"

"I mean it—beat it, will you? You might not be interested in running anymore, but Sandy is, and I'd rather not see you around bothering her."

This was a guy who had wanted *me* to work out there, and now he was trying to get rid of me. I was so annoyed by the way he'd spoken to me that I didn't even answer him, just turned and headed for my car. I figure I'd sit inside and get my homework done while Sandy ran. That way I'd have more time that evening to talk to her.

The time really dragged, but then it always does when I'm studying. When Sandy finally opened the door to the car and got inside I felt as though I'd been waiting for days instead of only hours.

"Why'd you leave?" she asked me.

"Your coach didn't want me around."

She didn't say anything to that. She didn't even stand up for me, so I figured he must have told her his reasons. I kept waiting for her to bring up the subject again as I drove her home, but she just chatted about how good it felt to be running again and what the coach was going to have her do to get her times down again.

"Did you hear me when I yelled at you about your arms?" I finally asked.

"Yeah, but that's nothing that can be helped right now. It's the added weight. The coach says as I slim down my arms will come down."

"You were pretty slow out there, waddling around the track," I said with a smile, kidding her.

Usually she would have just punched me in the arm or something, but instead she just sat in silence, her face lacking any expression at all when I glanced over at her.

"Hey, Sandy, I was only kidding."

"I've got to get this weight off fast" was all she said, but the way she said it, it sounded as though she was blaming me for putting on the extra weight. I might have been a little at fault—we did both go off that diet while she was resting her ankle—but she could've stuck to it if she'd wanted to.

We went to her house and worked out on her equipment, but it wasn't working out we were doing when her mom came home. She was sitting on my lap and giving me little kisses all over my face, and I felt pretty dumb when Mrs. Smith caught us at it.

"Sandy" was all she needed to say to get Sandy to jump quickly off my lap looking guilty.

"We've been working out, Mom," she said.

I could swear her mother was trying not to smile at that remark. She just looked at the two of us and said, "Well, enjoy yourselves while you can. Tomorrow you start at the gym."

"You got me in?" Sandy had a grin as wide as her face.

Her mom just nodded. "You'll go straight from Runners West to the gym. John's talked to your coach and they're coming up with a special program for you."

Her mom left the room and Sandy turned to me. "I've been trying to get in there for ages, but John was all booked up. I guess it's because of my ankle he probably feels I really need it now."

"Who's John?" was all I asked.

"You know the Naples Gym—John runs it. They even have a pool, and my coach says swimming will be good for getting my weight back down."

I was wondering whether I could swing the cost of a gym on my allowance. It wouldn't hurt to check it out, anyway, and I enjoyed swimming. I left pretty soon after that, telling Sandy I'd call her later. When I got home, I looked up the gym in the phone book and gave them a call, but I was told there were no openings.

"Would you like me to put your name on the waiting list?" a guy asked me.

"Do you know how long the wait will be?" I asked him.

"Probably several months."

I told him not to bother, then hung up. Well, so I wouldn't be seeing as much of Sandy anymore, that was all right. Finals would be coming up soon and I could use the extra time for studying. And I'd make sure the time we did have together was well spent. It might even do us some good to have a little breather from each other.

That night, when I called Sandy, she only talked with me for about five minutes before saying, "I've got to get back to my studying now, Tom. Mom thinks I ought to try to get ahead if I can as I'm not going to have much time from now on."

The next day, I drove her to practice after school and then sat around and waited for her, then drove her to the gym, and again sat around outside in my car and waited for her. I was beginning to feel like some kind of a chauffeur. That night when I called, her mom told me Sandy was back at the gym for swimming and suggested, nicely, that it might be better if the two of us didn't talk on the phone on school nights anymore. There wasn't much I could do but agree with her, you just don't talk back to your girlfriend's mother.

By the end of the week, though, I was getting pretty tired of the whole arrangement. The only time I was seeing Sandy was when we were in my car driving someplace. I hadn't even kissed her properly since Monday.

On Friday, when I drove her home from the gym, I asked her what she wanted to do that night.

"I have swimming, Tom," she said.

"On *Fridays*?"

"Seven nights a week."

"You're kidding!"

"And tomorrow I go back to ballet."

"What about your painting lessons?"

"I'm quitting; I won't have time for that anymore."

"But you were doing so well, Sandy, you shouldn't just give it up."

"It was fun when I didn't have anything else to do, but this is more important."

I was really sorry to hear that. Under the instruction of Michelle's mom, Sandy had been doing some really good watercolors and her mother had even had a couple framed and they now hung in their living room. Still, I could see her new schedule didn't allow for much else. I figured maybe once she got back into shape she'd go back to it.

"How about if I pick you up after swimming tonight and we'll go out?"

"I don't think so, Tom—I'll be too tired. Tomorrow night would be better; at least I can sleep in on Sundays."

I was relieved to hear that; I was beginning to think I'd be spending my Saturday nights alone.

When I picked Sandy up after swimming on Saturday night, her mom was there and she took me aside while Sandy was changing her clothes.

"I think it would be a good idea if you two cooled it for a while," she told me.

"What do you mean? I can't see her anymore?"

"She's got a lot of hard work ahead of her, Tom, if she wants to make a good showing in Helsinki. I'm sure you have a lot of things to do—you're graduating in a few weeks, aren't you?"

I nodded, wondering if this meant I couldn't see her at all. But surely Sandy had some say in her life, and seeing me once in a while, at least on Saturday nights, wasn't going to hurt her any. "I'd like to hear this from Sandy," I told her.

Mrs. Smith sighed. "Sandy asked me to mention it to you."

"Why didn't she tell me herself?"

"I think she's a little overwhelmed by you. You know she's never dated a boy before, and she's not very sure of herself where you're concerned. Anyway, we've talked it over, and Sandy agrees that getting back to normal will be best."

"Does this mean you'll be driving her to practice?" I asked.

I could see she was torn between wanting to get out of it herself and being fair to me. "I'll drive her," she said at last.

"What about Saturday nights?"

"I see no reason why you shouldn't go out occasionally. I don't think she should be totally deprived of a social life. When I was in high school..." She let the words trail off, leaving me wondering what had happened when she was in high school. Judging by how good she looked now, I figured she was probably really popular with the boys.

Sandy and I saw a movie that night and I didn't bring up the subject of seeing her until I had taken her home and we were parked in front of her house. Then I said, "Why'd you have your mother talk to me, Sandy? Why didn't you do it yourself?"

She didn't pretend not to know what I was talking about. "I didn't want you to get mad at me."

"I'm not mad at you, but I just think it would've been better coming from you. You're not a little kid anymore, Sandy—your mother can't do everything for you."

"You are mad, I can tell."

"Well, I've got to admit I'm not too happy about never seeing you anymore."

"You're seeing me now."

"One night a week? That's not very much, Sandy."

"What do you want from me, Tom? That's all the time I've got."

I thought we were getting very close to having a big fight, so I put out my arm along the back of the seat. That was the signal that she should move over in my arms, but she ignored it, just sat there staring stonily ahead of her.

That really got me angry. "Maybe we shouldn't see each other at all anymore," I said, thinking that she'd immediately move into my arms and tell me not to be so silly, that she wanted to see me whenever she could.

But all she said was, "Maybe we shouldn't."

I just sat there in a state of shock at those words. I barely even noticed when she got out of the car and went into her house. I couldn't believe she would just end it like that. Maybe I shouldn't have said what I did, but she could've given me an argument about it, couldn't she? Any other girl would've. But no, she just gets out of the car and leaves me like she'd never even cared.

I finally started up the car and headed for home. I was upset, really upset, but I didn't think it was actually over between us. I'd said the wrong thing, that's all, and out of some perversity she'd taken me up on it. But that wasn't the end, I was sure of it. I'd call her in the morning and tease her a little and everything would be okay again. It had to be, because I loved her too much to just let her go.

When I called her in the morning nobody answered. I stuck around the house all day, calling her about every five minutes, until finally I figured there was something wrong with their phone and I reported it to the phone company. But I was told there wasn't anything wrong, so I figured maybe they went somewhere for the day. Either that or she wasn't answering on purpose.

I finally got in my car and drove by her house. Her mother's car wasn't around, so I drove off and headed for Hamburger Henry's. I had myself a couple of burgers and some fries, then headed back to her house. I parked out in front for a while but she didn't show up, so finally I headed back home.

I watched TV with my folks that night and at about ten I went upstairs to my room and tried her number again. This time her mother answered and told me that Sandy was already in bed. I thanked her and hung up.

When I went to pick her up for school the next morning, she'd already left. For the next two days I tried to ignore her, put her out of my mind, but it just wasn't possible. I didn't look for her in the halls anymore, but at night I'd call her house and if she answered, I'd hang up. I didn't do it too often as I figured they'd know it was me and maybe get the number changed or something. But I just had to hear her voice. I would be sitting in my room trying to study and this overwhelming urge would come over me to hear her voice, and the next thing I knew I'd be dialing her number.

I started driving by her house a lot, too. That and Runners West and the gym. I didn't have much else to do and I like driving around, but a couple of times her mother spotted me, so after that I had to be more careful. I would park about a block away from her house, around the corner. Once, on Friday, I actually saw her and it was all I could do not to jump out of the car and run to her. I didn't, though.

I decided instead just to call her on Saturday and ask her out on a date. I figured all she could do was refuse, and that wasn't any worse than not trying at all.

I called her on Saturday afternoon, and when she answered I didn't hang up.

"Hi, Sandy, it's me," I said.

"Hello, Tom."

"Listen, I was wondering if you wanted to go out tonight. There's a good movie at the Belmont...."

"Thanks, but I can't."

"You can't or you won't?"

There was a pause. "I have a science project I have to work on this weekend."

"Need any help?"

"No, I can do it. It's just time-consuming, that's all."

"How've you been, anyway?"

"Fine."

I could tell from the tone of her voice that she didn't want to talk to me, that she was merely being polite. The whole conversation, in fact, was unnerving me, so I finally mumbled a goodbye and hung up.

I spent that night sitting in my room and looking at her pictures. I even read over the articles I had on her, although by then I practically knew them by heart. About nine I called her house and hung up when she answered. I felt ashamed of myself for acting like that, but if she hadn't done what she had, it wouldn't have been necessary. It just seemed such a waste that she was sitting over at her house all alone and I was all alone at mine. I'm sure she would've been a lot happier if we were together.

A little while later I called again, but the line was busy. I kept calling about every thirty seconds for an hour, but it was still busy, so I figured she'd taken the phone off the hook.

I was climbing the walls in my room by that time, so I got my car out and *drove* past her house. Their lights were on inside, so I parked and watched the windows. I was still there when her mom came home from her date about one in the morning, and when I saw them pull up I hunched down in my seat so they couldn't see me. I saw her mom kissing the guy good-night, then I stayed until I saw the lights go out.

I was in pretty bad shape that month. I couldn't concentrate at school, my studying was haphazard at best, and I knew I was being nasty to everyone at home. I snapped at Chrissie every time she said anything to me and barely said anything at all to my folks. They seemed to be understanding, so I guess they knew what had happened. I realized that Sandy's name was never being mentioned around the house—not by me, not by anyone.

One night in a fit of frustration, I began to rip Sandy's pictures off the wall in my room, tearing several of them in the process. Then I had regrets and spent the rest of the evening taping them back together. I didn't want to lose her completely, and I figured if I didn't have the pictures I wouldn't have anything.

That night, I wrote my first letter to her. I had to communicate with her in some way, and since talking to her was out...

I'd never written a letter to a girl before and wasn't sure I could even do it. But once I started, the words just seemed to flow, and soon I had several pages of notebook paper covered with my indecipherable handwriting. Mostly, I just told her how I felt about her and reminded her of all the good times we'd had. Toward the end of it, though, I was pleading for her to see me again, at least once.

When I finished it, I recopied it carefully so she'd be able to read every word. Then I put it in an envelope, got one of

Mom's stamps to put on it, and walked down to the mail-box. It made me feel good, as if I was really making an effort. It also helped in that I felt I was actually talking to Sandy while I wrote to her.

By the time I got back home I was thinking of all kinds of things I could've said, so I got into bed and began writing her another. This one was more of a love letter, really. I thought maybe the next day I'd go to the shopping mall and buy her one of those funny cards and put the letter inside it. I was feeling a whole lot better about everything when I went to bed that night.

The next day I went to the mall, and they had so many cards I liked I couldn't decide on just one of them, so I bought about a dozen. I also saw a stuffed animal I would've liked to send to her, but I didn't have enough money with me to buy it. It was a bear wearing a running suit, and the more I thought about it, the more I thought she'd like it. So I went home and got my next week's allowance and went back and blew it all on the bear. The girl in the store put it in a box for me and even wrapped it for mailing. I wouldn't have any lunch money for the week, but I needed to take off some weight anyway. And I could use my lunch hour the next day to take the box down to the post office. I thought of driving over and leaving it on her doorstep, but I figured it would be more impressive coming in the mail.

So I sent the bear and I sent the cards and I waited all week for Sandy to come up to me at school and say something, or at least call me at home. But she didn't. I began to picture the bear sitting on her bed and wondered if she thought about me whenever she saw him. I kept writing letters, thinking she'd break down and talk to me soon, but before long I couldn't think of anything clever to say and they were just becoming pleas for her to see me again. Then I got a picture in my mind of her and her mother laughing over them, so I stopped. I didn't stop writing them, but I stopped mailing them to her.

The senior prom was coming up; after the dance all the kids went to Disneyland, which they kept open all night just for that evening. When my mom asked me if I was going, I said I didn't know. I didn't really think it would do any good to call Sandy and ask her, so I decided to write her one more letter. In it, I told her how much it would mean to me if she'd go with me, and I also told her how much fun it would be. I figured the Disneyland part would interest her even if *I* didn't; all the kids love going to Disneyland.

I told her she didn't even have to call me and give me an answer. I included a postcard in the letter on which she could just check off yes or no and mail it back to me. Then I waited around waiting for an answer. Every day I'd rush home from school to see if the card had arrived, but it never did. When I knew she was never going to answer, I decided she was probably right not to. I was getting a little old for Disneyland and senior proms were silly.

I was so obsessed with thoughts of Sandy that I forgot all about my birthday. When mom brought out my cake after dinner one night I was amazed that it was for me. I tried to act excited about the cake and all the presents, and everyone was acting really jolly, but it was probably the worst birthday I ever had. My dad said something about my being a man now, but I didn't feel any different than I had the day before. It was a joke anyway. In California, you can't even legally drink until you're twenty-one, so what's the big deal about being eighteen?

"What happened to Sandy?" Chrissie asked me that night. I was surprised she hadn't asked before; Chrissie usually isn't so subtle.

"She's busy getting back into shape," I told her.

"Too busy to even call you?"

"Quit hassling me, Chrissie."

"I'm not hassling you. I only asked you a simple question, that's all."

"Yeah, real simple—like you!"

I could see the tears start up in her eyes. I hardly ever talked to her mean like that, but I couldn't even find the decency to apologize. I was so upset about Sandy and me that nothing else seemed important anymore.

"No need to take it out on your sister," my dad said to me, and that made me so angry I went up to my room and slammed the door and didn't come out the rest of the night. I knew how childish I was acting. They'd tried to make it a nice birthday for me and I'd acted like a little kid who doesn't get his own way. That's what falling in love with a girl will do to you, I guess. I just wasn't acting rationally anymore.

We got our graduation invitations that week and I mailed one off to Sandy. I knew she wouldn't go but I wanted her to get the formal announcement, to realize that I wouldn't be in school with her next year and that she might not even see me again.

That week I also started sitting with Kenny in the cafeteria again. He sat with a group of other guys now, but I just went up and sat with them. The first time I did it, Kenny said to me, "Haven't seen you with Sandy lately, what's happening?"

"Well, you know, she's pretty busy getting back into shape."

"You seeing her at all?"

I almost started to lie to him, then instead I said, "No. I guess we've broken up."

"What do you mean you guess? Don't you know?"

"Yeah, it's all over."

Then I started to talk to him about it and pretty soon the other guys at the table got bored, I guess, and left. But Kenny sat there and listened to me. He didn't give me any advice, but he was a good listener.

"What should I do?" I asked him, when I'd told him all the pertinent facts.

"Why don't you try calling her and talking about it?"

"She won't talk to me."

"You could maybe write her."

"I have."

He shook his head. "I don't know, Tom, I guess it's really over then. You'll just have to get over her."

"How do you get over someone, Tom?"

"Maybe Michelle could tell you."

I guess he saw how stung I felt by his words, because he quickly added, "Sorry about that. That was a pretty low blow, I guess."

"I've been pretty stupid, huh?" I asked him.

"Everyone's entitled to be stupid once in a while."

It had been such a relief talking about Sandy to someone that I started calling Kenny on the phone at night so I'd be able to talk about her. I could tell I was starting to bore him, though, and it wasn't too many calls before he started telling me he had to go somewhere, or he had studying to do, and in the cafeteria he looked as bored as his friends when I'd start up. So after a while I started eating by myself again and quit calling him at all.

I briefly thought about asking another girl to the prom, but I figured all the ones I'd want to take would already be going. That's not the kind of thing you ask a girl to at the last minute, anyway. Also, I knew I wouldn't be very good company for any date. I'd be wishing I were with Sandy all night and that wouldn't be fair. And even if I could, I didn't want to get interested in another girl. What was the point if things could end up so unhappily? I'd rather just go on loving Sandy from a distance than taking a chance on getting hurt again.

I should have been spending my time studying for my finals, but I couldn't get interested. Anyway, I wouldn't flunk though I'd probably get low grades. The night of the senior prom I tried to do a little studying, but I soon gave it up and just sat there thinking what a good time I could have had with Sandy. I found myself wondering if Michelle was there. But of course she would be; Mike Stern was a senior and as far as I knew they were still going together.

I could hardly even remember Michelle now; she seemed like someone from another life. I felt sorry for her, though, because now I knew how she must've felt when we broke up. Only she couldn't have possibly felt as bad as I did or she wouldn't have started dating so soon. Unless she did that in an attempt to make me jealous.

It made me wonder if maybe Sandy would get jealous if she started seeing me with another girl, but I decided she wouldn't. Sandy just wasn't the jealous type. But if she had really loved me, wouldn't she be? Wouldn't it only be normal? But I didn't want to think those kind of thoughts because then I might start wondering if she'd ever really loved me at all. And if she hadn't, then I'd wasted an entire year for no reason at all.

Chapter Ten

I graduated in June and the day couldn't come quickly enough for me. I wanted to be finished with high school, never have to see the place again. I had good memories of it, really good memories, but they weren't of the past year. I had thought that during my senior year everything would come together: my studies, my social life, my running. But instead, the entire year had been taken up by some unrealistic dream I had of Sandy.

Needless to say, Sandy didn't come to my graduation, although if it had been hers I would have been there bearing gifts. My parents and Chrissie came, of course, and a few other assorted relatives, and they were all bearing gifts, but it wasn't gifts I was interested in, it was getting out of Wilson High and starting over in college. I vowed that in college I'd follow my head rather than my heart.

Diploma in hand, I walked over to where I was supposed to meet my folks after the graduation ceremony, then stopped when I saw they were talking to Michelle. I knew she hadn't come to see *me* graduate; Mike Stern was also graduating. I also knew my folks had always liked her and that it had been mutual, so I gave them a couple of minutes to talk before letting Michelle catch sight of my impending arrival. I thought she deserved a chance to get away from me if that was her choice.

She was looking good again. She'd put back the weight she'd lost and was dressed in a short pink dress with a low neck; the color really set off her dark hair. She was still the prettiest girl in the school. From a distance, I could see the sun bouncing off something around her neck, and for a moment I thought she was still wearing the silver heart I had given her, but up close I saw that it had been replaced by a conch shell crafted in silver.

Instead of rushing off, she said hello to me, and from the look in her clear eyes I could tell that any bitterness she had felt for me was now over with and that I was nothing more to her now than an old friend. Or maybe not even a friend.

She asked me what my plans were for the summer, and I told her I didn't have any as yet, but that I'd be looking around for a job. I asked her the same, and learned that she had a job as a crafts instructor at a summer camp in the mountains. It seemed that everyone was going to the mountains for the summer but me.

Then Mike came over to claim her, and I stood by while Michelle introduced him to my parents. I could see Chrissie looking from Mike to me and wondering what Michelle saw in Mike, but maybe that's just what I wanted her to be thinking. In actuality, Mike's a good-looking guy, and he also looked in much better shape than I was at that moment. I'd gone back to junk food with a vengeance, and that combined with the lack of exercise had added a few extraneous pounds to my body. Nothing I couldn't take off with some running, but I hadn't been motivated to run lately.

A week after graduation, on a Saturday, I found my car heading in the direction of Sandy's house. I still drove by there occasionally. It wasn't something I thought about or even planned to do. It was as if my car knew the right directions to take to get there. All I had to do was sit back and soon I'd be cruising through Naples and slowing down when I got to her house. It was a quiet street, and I seldom saw anyone outside their houses and never saw Sandy, but this day was different.

There was a moving van parked in front of their house, and Mrs. Smith was directing two men who were carrying furniture and cartons out of the house. I didn't take in what I was seeing at first. When I did, I parked my car and got out and walked back to the house. Mrs. Smith said hello to me and asked me how I'd been, but it wasn't pleasantries I was interested in.

"You're moving?" I asked. Not that I couldn't see for myself.

"Didn't Sandy tell you?"

I shook my head. "No, but I haven't seen much of her lately."

She frowned. "But we've known for months."

The shock of her words was slowly sinking in. "Where're you moving to?"

"Eugene, Oregon. There's a coach up there who's very interested in working with Sandy."

"What about your job?

She gave small smile. "I can sell real estate just as well up there, I expect. If not...well, I can always do office work."

"When exactly did you decide to move?"

"April, as I recall. Sandy's inside if you want to see her, Tom."

April? Sandy had known about the move in *April*? In other words, the entire time I thought everything was perfect with us, when she was telling me she loved me and was seeing me daily, she already knew she'd be moving to Oregon in the summer and had never said a word about it to me. I stood there rooted to the spot as I thought about the implications of her having that knowledge.

I don't know whether it would have changed anything if she had told me, perhaps not. But I probably would have looked into that job as a lifeguard had I known she wouldn't be around for the summer. No, that probably wasn't true. More likely, I would have planned somehow to be able to spend the summer in Oregon to be near her. I might even have tried to get into the university nearby. Unlike Kenny, I hadn't been offered a track scholarship there, but I would have been accepted academically.

My good sense was telling me not to walk into the house, to forget about Sandy and never see her again. But some other part of me took over, told me at least I could see her one last time, and I found my legs moving up the walk, climbing the two stairs to her front door, then walking inside. She wasn't in the living room so I headed back to her bedroom.

Surrounded by cartons, she was transferring her clothes from her closet into a wardrobe made of cardboard. She was thin again, which made her look younger, and I stood there for a moment watching her. Then, "Hello, Sandy."

"Tom!" She turned around and smiled and I could've sworn she was glad to see me.

"You're moving, I see."

"To Oregon. Oh, Tom—I'm so excited; all the good runners are up there."

"How've you been Sandy?"

She looked around at the cartons. "Busy. It's hard work moving, it really is."

"But how have *you* been?"

"Busy. You know my schedule."

"Are you happy, Sandy?"

"What a question! Of course I'm happy."

She looked happy. She sounded happy. There probably wasn't anything important enough to her to mar that happiness unless it was to do with her running. That seemed to be her whole life, just as I had tried to make her my whole life. I had a feeling then that if I told her I still loved her, she'd say, "I love you, too, Tom," just the way she'd say it about chocolate ice cream if I said it first. It was just a word she used for things she liked. She didn't need words to express how she felt about running; she simply devoted her entire life to it.

It was difficult not to tell her once again how I felt about her, but I knew the meaning of it would go clear over her head. The urge to take her in my arms one last time was strong, too, but instead I shoved my hands in the pockets of my jeans and said to her, "Good luck, Sandy. I expect I'll be reading about you in the papers."

"I have a meet next weekend in San Luis Obispo. Will you be coming?"

I thought about it. It was only a few hours' drive up the coast. Pretty country, I wouldn't mind seeing it again. I would sit by myself in the stands waiting for her event, waiting with thousands of others who'd been drawn there by her skill, her celebrity. There would be an initial hush when she appeared, then the people in the stands would act as one, exploding into the kind of screaming and cheering reserved for starts. And then, as thousands of pairs of eyes followed her swift progress around the tract, I'd be holding my breath, willing her on. And she would win, of course. As of yet, there was no one who could beat her. Her happiness was undoubtedly assured for several years to come. But right now it was my happiness I was concerned with and seeing her just one more time wasn't going to do me any good at all. I knew I wouldn't soon forget her, but the sooner I started making an effort in the direction the better it was going to be for me.

"No, I don't think I'll be coming, Sandy," I told her, looking closely at her face for any signs of disappointment. There was none.

"Well, wish me luck, Tom." And those were the last words she ever spoke to me.

I drove home slowly and went straight to my room. I had some moving of my own to do, specifically the removing of her pictures from my walls. I took them down slowly, sometimes pausing to read what had been written beneath the pictures, then shoving them in to my wastebasket. I didn't need the pictures anyway; it wasn't likely I'd forget how she looked.

When only the framed magazine cover remained, I took it down slowly, then set it aside. Maybe Chrissie would like it for her room. It might be that Sandy would be the only celebrity she'd ever know personally. I carried it into her room and put it on her desk. She could keep it or throw it out, it made no difference to me.

I carried my wastebasket out to the garage and emptied the contents into a trash barrel. I didn't want any second thoughts about what I was doing. She was out of my life now and there was no longer any reason to be reminded of her each time I entered my room.

When I went back to my room my walls looked bare, but it no longer seemed the prison it had become in past weeks. Feeling unaccountably as though a weight had been lifted off me, I changed into my running shoes and shorts and headed for the beach. It was time to get back into shape again. Time to get back to normal.

The Silhouette Cameo Tote Bag Now available for just $6.99

Handsomely designed in blue and bright pink, its stylish good looks make the Cameo Tote Bag an attractive accessory. The Cameo Tote Bag is big and roomy (13″ square), with reinforced handles and a snap-shut top. You can buy the Cameo Tote Bag for $6.99, plus $1.50 for postage and handling.

Send your name and address with check or money order for $6.99 (plus $1.50 postage and handling), a total of $8.49 to:

**Silhouette Books
120 Brighton Road
P.O. Box 5084
Clifton, NJ 07015-5084
ATTN: Tote Bag**

SIL-T-1R

The Silhouette Cameo Tote Bag can be purchased pre-paid only. No charges will be accepted. Please allow 4 to 6 weeks for delivery.

N.Y. State Residents Please Add Sales Tax

Offer not available in Canada.

First Love from Silhouette

THE MOST POPULAR TEEN ROMANCES PUBLISHED TODAY

The books that you have enjoyed all these years with characters so real they seem like friends, and stories so engrossing that you have begged for more!

4 TITLES A MONTH

Stories that mirror your hopes, your dreams, your relationships — the books that you have claimed as your own ever since we first published them.

First Love from Silhouette

FL-A-1